I0719471

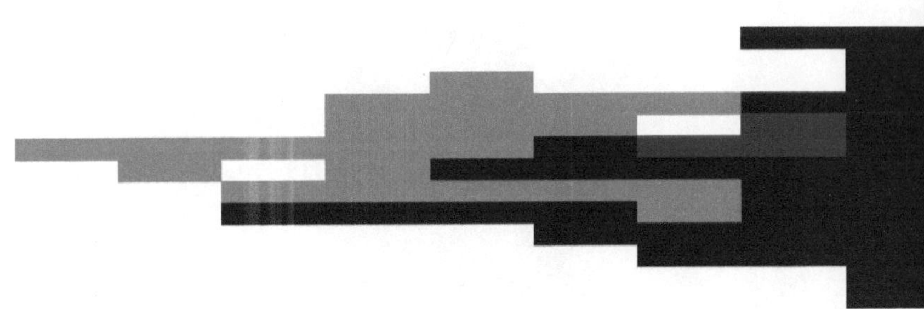

SIGHTSEER

THE PLASTIC FANTASTIC BOOK 1

SIGHTSEER

DEAN VALE

NOSETOUCH PRESS

CHICAGO • PITTSBURGH • MMXXV

SIGHTSEER

THE PLASTIC FANTASTIC BOOK 1

ISBN-13: 978-1-944286-52-1
Paperback Edition

Published by Nosetouch Press
www.nosetouchpress.com

For more information, contact Nosetouch Press:
info@nosetouchpress.com

This book is a work of fiction. Names, characters, places, and incidents either are products of the authors imaginations or are used fictitiously. Any resemblance to actual persons, living or dead, events, or locales is entirely coincidental.

Cataloging-in-Publication Data

Names: Vale, Dean., author.
Title: Sightseer
Description: Chicago, IL : Nosetouch Press [2025]
Identifiers: ISBN: 9781944286521(paperback)
Subjects: LCSH: Science—Fiction. | Cyberpunk fiction.
GSAFD: Science fiction.
BISAC: FICTION / Science Fiction / Cyberpunk

Cover & interior designed by Christine M. Scott, clevercrow.com

FOR MY BOYS

TABLE OF CONTENTS

TABLE OF CONTENTS

SIGHTSEER

THE EYES HAVE IT

Answers came through like questions in Shytown, as full of mystery and opportunity as circumstances allowed. In this case, it was Cam Sexton's third visit to Doculus in the Vision District in as many years. He was in search of an upgrade that would help him stand out among his rivals. In the meantime, outside, it rained. It always rained, the wounded sky forever crying toxic tears.

Shytown glowed like the steel-and-neon Heartland amethyst that it had been for as long as anyone with historical memory remembered. With Chillwaukee to the north, the Hinterland to the west, and the Shambles to the east, Shytown was part postindustrial fortress, part metaphysical sanctuary for the desperate and ruthless. With the Great Lake fervently licking its toes along the shore, Shytown had nothing to answer for, no one to answer to. It was both haven and heaven for its inhabitants, a place of refuge and risk, of ecstasy and despair.

Like all of the remaining cities worth the name, Shytown was overtly garbed in trideo and holographic garments, shooting ads into the skies and all across its busy streets. No one who lived there had any doubt where they stood, dreaming while awake, tossing in their coffinlike dwellings, illuminated by blue, pink, green, yellow, saffron, and more hues than ordinary eyes might see.

Doc Wellington was in, of course. He was constantly there. Doc was plastic handsome—chiseled chin and carbon-colored brush-cut hair, a don't-mess-with-me body that was probably vat-grown from the Midtown Body Politique and had to have cost him a fortune in scrip, chits, chips, goods, favors, and/or services. Such was the nature of augmentation.

Cam didn't care about any of that. He caught his reflection in one of the trideo ads that promised a better life on Mars, the auburn shades and pink-cheeked colonists in extraplanetary-appropriate attire promising a better life in seductive whispers. Just young enough not to be considered old, Cam had a natural handsomeness that hadn't come from a surgeon's scalpel—strong chin, an unbroken nose, high cheekbones, and an Imperial Purple™-colored pompadour that he trekked to Midtown to get refreshed monthly. His ever-present armored black leather jacket and grey slacks paired well with his polysteel-toed black work shoes, as did his rectangular ballistic mirrored sunglasses—which he wore not to protect his eyes from the absentee sun but served to disguise what he might be looking at. Every Looker owed that to themselves.

Beneath the red neon light of the unblinking eye of Doculus, dripping drops of acid rain, he'd come with wicked intent and plenty of scrip.

Wellington's office was a slender, monochromatic rectangle with three sales kiosks at the front, and a back area marked off with an opaque, holographic-shimmery metaplastic sheet that offered patients the naked pretense of privacy. The front door was armored, which only made sense. A mounted autogun watched that door with malevolently unwavering attention, the black gazing ball of its solitary camera eye perched above a 10mm smartgun over a red-painted sign that said "Don't be stupid" in five languages—English, Mandarin, Polish, Sanscript, and Russian.

The walls were lined with holographic eyes that blinked and beckoned with come hither glances. Cam wasn't here for those. These were tourist eyes. Cosmetic eye surgery was commonplace in Shytown and elsewhere, once the augmentation technology became more readily available. As a result, plenty of tourists secured the eyes they wanted at reasonable rates.

For Lookers, however, the choice of cybereyes was a matter of livelihood, life, and death. No Looker could afford to blink when it came to their choice in optics. What they saw, who they saw, how they saw all mattered to their audiences.

The Spliff looked annoyed at Cam from his berth in Booth Two. Cam caught his own reflection and could only agree. He *was* being intrusive. A more genteel sort of grovelingly desperate streetwalker would have at least waited until Doc was done making his pitch. But as he surveyed his silver shades protecting his most valuable assets in one of Doc's many mirrors, Cam was inclined to admit that he did not like to wait. Waiting was for Spliffs.

"Back so soon, Cam?" Doc asked, looking up from the bald, head-tatted, stone-faced Spliff he was upselling on intracranial optical packages.

"Not a complaint, Doc," Cam said. "Not with this one, anyway."

"A satisfied patient," Doc said. "Are you live? Can I get a testimonial from you?"

In Cam's world, there were Spliffs, Spiffs, Squiffs, Stiffs, Squids, and Strivers.

Spliffs were the hapless, hopeless wannabes who would never amount to anything, no matter how hard they tried. Spiffs were the swells, ones who had money and means, often imagined but seldom seen. Squiffs were the shaky ones, the freaks who looked ripe for a fall, whether through happenstance and/or self-medicated madness. They could be found anywhere, at any time, but were mostly Streetside. Stiffs were the workaday mundanes, overwhelmingly represented in megacorporate circles, or else they were corpses—sometimes they were both, if they messed up. Midtown was the native habitat of the Stiff. Squids were the criminal class, the ones who were mucking around in everybody else's biz, always approached with caution. While Squids were everywhere in the underground, they could be found Streetside, in Midtown, and Upperton. The higher a Squid went, the more dangerous they were sure to be. And the Strivers were the wealthy tryhards, one cyberslip away from ignominious oblivion. Strivers were most often identified by their anxious hustling, and how many of them came to messy ends. Most everybody fell within these classifications. He had everyone he knew filed that way, for ease of use. The terms could be compliments or insults, depending on the circumstance and setting.

An Eyewitness by trade (known as a Looker on the street), Cam broadcast to his audience whatever he saw. He was live more often than he was not, and his clients tracked his daily life with the hope that he'd see something interesting. Cam had made it his business to be as interesting as possible, getting into situations that might draw eyes and engagement. They rewarded him with attention and the attendant scrip that this attention provided. His work had made his feed the third most popular among the elite Lookers, with several million onlookers around the world tracking what he did as if it mattered.

Cam's segmented his audience by degree of interface, with more play for those willing to pay, the breakdown as follows, using terms he never shared with anyone else:

VOYEURS (5 percent): Strictly trideo feed, black and white, no audio. Why people opted for the silent black and white was something he could never figure out, but assumed there was some neo-noir lowball vibe to it that appealed for the price point. Some of the fancier drug dens would play that Voyeur feed for patrons as background visuals, as well as armored arthouses eager to convey an artistic flair. Plenty of drugged-out stim junkies would work that feed while they were tripping in whatever flop they inhabited. The Voyeurs were a small but strangely dedicated minority part of his audience.

ONLOOKERS (50 percent): Full-color trideo feed with audio. This was the single biggest segment of his audience, the technicolor tourists who were along for the ride and wanted to see as much as they could afford to observe. They could tune in live or get replays at their leisure. A ton of commentary came from Onlookers, with the more engaged ones being some of the chattiest on the feed.

PEEPERS (30 percent): Full-color trideo audiovisual feed with empathic/emotional interlink. These were among the more fervid members of his audience, who had thrown down for the empathic modules that let them feel what Cam was feeling. Some of his more obsessive and ardent fans were Peepers, and Cam happily mined that audience for dates, dalliances, and diversions.

CREEPERS (15 percent): Full-color trideo with audiovisual and empathic/emotional feeds and ability to chat with Cam in real-time. The VIPs of his audience, the Creepers had invested the most in his Looker status and felt a proprietary claim to his time and attention. As Creepers invariably had the best interlink rigs and the play money to spend on him, Cam was always willing to indulge them, including one-on-one sessions, if they paid enough for it.

There were plenty of Lookers out there, but none of them had the finesse that Cam did, or the audacity, or the audience share. He was pleased that he had an instinct for it, a nose for news, as it were, and a desire to chase down the sights that were worth seeing. Cam was willing to put himself at risk for the sake of his audience, and they loved him for it, as much as they were capable of loving anything.

That kind of tenacity often got Lookers killed, their body parts bought and sold by the Ghouls who patrolled the streets with startling regularity in their black vans with the white-painted gearhead skulls on their sides. The cops didn't even pretend to police the Ghouls, provided they kicked up to them without hesitation. From the perspective of the authorities, the Ghouls kept the streets clean—or at least free of bodies.

The Triads and Yaks condoned it, provided they got their cut. The way it always went with them. You paid, you played. It was part of the Shytown ecosystem, a sea of outstretched hands taking their respective cuts.

"I'm not live, Doc," Cam said, giving his hair a light tousle with the tritanium comb he always carried. The caustic raindrops blended in with each pass of the comb.

"Then why are you here?" Doc asked.

Cam nodded at the holographic poster showing the Imagix Eyeronic 777, the happy-pretty model with the bright blue eyes. The Spliff followed Cam's gaze. He looked back at him with rising irritation. Way out of his price range. The fact that Doc even had the poster on his wall was a status indicator.

"You already have those, Cam," Doc said.

"I want what you're *not* advertising," Cam said. "Rumor has it that you have something special. The TeleVista Eyeconic 360s."

At mention of them out loud, Doc got furtive, glancing around at no one in particular to be sure they didn't overhear. Even the Spliff seemed momentarily impressed.

"Rumors," Doc said.

"Oniyaki told me," Cam said. Just saying the young Yak's name got Doc even more nervous. But at least it had gotten his attention. He toggled the autoseller on the Booth Two kiosk and let the holographic nano-nanny talk the Spliff through the process, her sweetly subliminal voice soothing any concerns the guy may have had.

"You're serious, Cam?" Doc asked, walking up to him. Cam was taller than Doc, but not by much. Cam was tall, something he'd done nothing to deserve, but which he used to his advantage whenever he could, which was almost always. People looked up to Cam because they had to. Growing up in Midtown, Cam assumed it was because his parents had relatively good corporate gigs at Yougenix, where they worked in Biomarketing, and he'd had access to decent enough food to grow up halfway healthy. His dad had been an executive, while his mom had been a Yougenix corporate Looker.

Cam's mother was larger-than-life within Yougenix, where her corporate Lookerism ensured internal cohesion with the company's mission statement and messaging.

"The biotechnicians at Yougenix are working day and night to bring a better you to the market," his mom said. Always sharply-dressed in the Yougenix company colors of blue and red, his mom would snake her way throughout the company lairs and research centers, guided by her handlers and an impeccable editing runner team offering real-time feed updates.

He'd never really seen much of them, since they were intended for Yougenix employees, contractors, and clients. As a result, company privacy and property agreements kept them out of the eyelines of competitors and others. What he'd glanced at as a kid gave him the idea of what she did without the substance.

Cam thought he looked like her, which probably helped in his later efforts. His father was of sterner stuff, tall and lean, with silver hair and a hard cerulean gaze.

"We're paving the trail for you, Cam," his father said. "Your mother and me. Never forget that. Yougenix is a family. And you're part of that family, too."

Living in Midtown with the other Striver families, Cam never had a reason to doubt that family sentiment. The elevated life brought plentiful fun and frolic, with Streetside being something he looked down on from the comfort and relative safety of the Pedway. The company kids had their logo patches and pins that meant they were monitored by corp security and didn't have to worry about being more than targets of corporate agents, should things go bad. One push on the panic button and deliverance was at hand, or else.

Midtown living meant climate-controlled life under ballistic glass. Few Midtowners would tolerate the open air, and many of them had nanomasks in their briefcases. For Cam, it created a strange alienation from the wider world, something that translated into his Looker work that came later.

"I've got the scrip for it," Cam said. "I wanted to see if you still had them."

"Of course I do," Doc said. "But I just got you the Imag-ix Eyeronic 777s last year, Cam. You can't have worn them out already. If they had a warranty, you'd still be under it."

"Whatever," Cam said. "Scrip is scrip, Doc. Chit happens. I want the 360s."

Doc was intrigued by this. He tightly pursed his picture-perfect lips.

"Spill," Doc said, grabbing himself a hot cup of Synthostim™, offering one to Cam, who turned it down with a wave of his hand.

"I'm getting some dropoff on the back nine," Cam said, watching his friend sip his stim. He preferred pills and derms and thought the liquid stims were for tourists and twankers. "Audience seepage. Gapers and gogglers bouncing. I'm losing market share."

"I don't see how," Doc said.

"I don't, either," Cam said. "But it's making a dent, and I want better resolution. I want state of the art. Nobody else has the Eyeconics. Nobody at my level, anyway. Not Victor Glimpse in Midtown or Sandra Scene slumming it in Upperton. They're running the table with access, but I want something full spectrum. I want to be seen at *any* scene, if you know what I mean."

The Lookers were always jockeying for position. Sandra Scene's *Scene Be Seen* took advantage of her high-profile Upperton upbringing and rampant insider connections to give her a window into the everyday elite who lived above the clouds. She jealously guarded her cyberspace with her artful entourage escapades and sexual safaris, and her loyal audience ate it up.

Victor Glimpse held Midtown's gaze, made his scrip with *Lingering Glimpse,* where he availed himself of the megacorporate Stiffs who were willing to use his eyes to get whatever message out the multinationals wanted to send that day. It was rock-steady work that Cam almost envied, but he thought Glimpse was always the laziest of the Lookers, preferring the stories to come to him than the other way around. Not that Glimpse reminded him of his mother, but that kind of megacorp work left Cam cold.

In contrast, Cam was the Prince of the Pavement, preferring to stay Streetside, where he considered everything to be far more real. Let Sandra gloat and float on her clouds, let Glimpse navigate the pedways in his PR flak jacket—Cam's own *Sightseer* feed was where it was at. He'd taken shots the others wouldn't have gone near, and he never blinked when it mattered.

Doc downed his syntho and poured another. For one in his work, his steady nerves and steadier hands meant everything. Syntho drips meant fewer slips.

"You talk to Wren about this?" Doc asked. Cam time-shared with Oniyaki, while street detective Wren and his band of badges formed up the other major part of his client commitment. It was one of the arrangements he'd made after jettisoning his Midtown life.

For a Looker, what mattered was cultivating people who saw things worth seeing and didn't mind sharing. Cam cut both Wren and Oniyaki in on his take, and it worked out well enough for all parties involved. From Cam's vantage point, Streetside was where it was at, where the blend of blood, sweat, and desperation fueled rash acts that made for great audience action.

"I haven't," Cam said. "But I don't see Wren having a problem with it."

"Alright," Doc said. "I don't want to do this and have him beating down my door and taking any fingers."

"No worries, Doc," Cam said. "As I see it, you can take the 777s on resale, give them to somebody like Spliffo over there, and nobody's the wiser. You give me the 360s and suddenly I'm bleeding edge, without an unnecessary drop spilled."

Doc got almost wistful at the thought of them, his syntho giving him a little drymouth. Whatever one might say about Doc, he loved his work the way he loved nothing else.

"Yeah," Doc said. "They are that. Nobody trades in eyes anymore. Not like they used to. When I started out, *everybody* wanted them. Nowadays, it's all other stuff—hearts and minds, legs, arms, backs, you know what I mean? Who knew being clearsighted had a shelf life?"

"Sure, sure," Cam said. "I'm what you'd call a new traditionalist, Doc. I see, therefore I am."

"Ever the poet-philosopher, Cam. The tradvertising has sunk its teeth in you is my guess," Doc said. "You come by at midnight, we'll get you sorted out. Half up front?"

Cam had come prepared. He'd even brought a case. He'd sweated lugging it through Downertown, had expected someone would try to jack him for it. The smart move would've been coming with a bodyguard, but Cam thought incognito was the better way to go. Certainly more affordable. As a Looker, Cam knew when being hard to spot was necessary. He knew from personal experience that even the best bodyguards didn't keep someone safe.

The last time he saw his parents, his father looked particularly tense. Cam could see him trying to disguise it, putting up a stony confidence to disguise his level of concern. The blue suit he wore, the Yougenix pin at his lapel, the matching cufflinks—the man radiated corporate meta-confidence, which was one part terror, one part ruthlessness. His mother looked amazing in her red dress, emblazoned with the company logo, her cybereyes shining, her team walking in her wake, as she made the latest

Yougenix PR jaunt seem like a gracious and gallant outing as they worked their way to the company hovercar.

It was a special trip, because his father had been promoted to Vice President of Biomarketing, and his mom was the one tapped to cover it as they were set to meet with Phantasonic's Biomarketing team, in what was widely suspected would be a possible company merger. The two megacorporations were heavily involved in the cybernetic and biotechnological industries.

Finia, the company bodyguard for the family, told Cam as much. She doubled as a sort of nanny, although her sleek features and jet-black, short hair and predatory-sharp build always made her seem edgier than more typical caregivers.

"This is a big day, Cam," Finia said. "Should your dad work this deal, you're all bound for Upperton. We're talking orbital. The Heights."

"Really?" Cam asked. Finia nodded. She stood near him, giving him his space, but Cam knew from experience that she was watching everything that was going on. The wraparound shades she wore hid her own cybereye rig, scaled for bodyguard details. Most of those were trade-secretive, but Cam had researched on his own, knew there were targeting algorithms, as well as facial recognition software with interlink capabilities with a host of companies. Few ever got the drop on Finia.

So, when the Yougenix hovercar was blown apart by high-velocity weapons fire that came from several angles, Finia was quick to react, even as Cam was stunned. She grabbed him, one streamlined arm hooking under his arm and spiriting him away as the overhead explosion sent shrapnel raining down on the launchpad.

"This is Finisher to Dispatch," Finia said. "We're under fire here. The package has been dropped."

Finia moved with nerve-attenuated speed, so that Cam could barely see what was happening—it being a percussive, pyrotechnic blur. The hovercar had crashed to the helipad, further detonating, and Cam could see the black, unmarked attack helicopters hovering in silhouette like wasps, peeling off, having accomplished their mission, racing off for parts unknown.

"You okay, Cam?" Finia asked, her lips near his ear.

"My parents," Cam replied, stammering it out, blinking tears.

"Yeah," Finia said, holding him tightly. "No."

He handed over the case to Doc, who glanced at the Spliff, who was still absorbed in his presentation, having donned the silver oculus crescent visor that was offering him a simulated view of what he might be seeing with his new eyes. Cam knew from personal experience how immersive those could be.

Doc opened the case and gazed at the piles of periwinkle scrip greeting him, arranged in orderly banded stacks. Few things were as immediately persuasive as fat stacks of scrip and chits. They took people to special places, made them inclined to do hasty, reckless things.

"This is a thing of beauty, Cam," Doc said, running his steady hands over them. "And you're such a gentleman to pay in cash. How thoughtfully discreet of you."

Cam smiled at Doc, a fetching smile he knew could move mountains. He'd watched his mom practice her smile for years, had tried to do his own masculine version of it, and had been pleased whenever it worked for him. In Shytown, smiles were both magnetic locks and keys, able to give one a pass to unseen places, or could deflect the unwelcome when needed.

"I trust you for it," Cam said. "Friendship has its privileges."

"Absolutely," Doc said, snapping shut the case and sliding it into his autosafe behind his armored desk. "You bring the rest, and you've got your eyes."

"Let me see them," Cam said. "I want to see."

"Of course you do," Doc said, fishing out the TeleVista case from the autosafe, the logo showing an eye gazing from a mountain triangle, sending out beams like sunrays. He opened them and showed off the optical implants, the diamond-hard double orbs with the autocolored irises currently set to green. Cam reached out to touch them, only to have Doc swat his fingerless gloved hands away. "They're not yours yet, Cam."

He closed the case and secured them in the autosafe. There was no point in arguing with Doc about them, as they weren't his, yet.

"The Eyeconic 360s offer infrared, ultraviolet, lowlight, thermographic, flashguard, targeting optics, SeeThru™ as well," Doc said. "10x binocular zoom, black and white, color, full interface with optilink and highly scratch resistant. The variable iris color option is standard, and you get HUD interface, naturally."

"Naturally," Cam said. He could hardly wait. "How'd a street rat like yourself get such choice optics?"

Doc pretended to be insulted, and his face would've wrinkled if his pricy elective cosmetic work would have permitted it. Doc had come from some kind of money, or else was a particularly ravenous wheeler-dealer. Based on his professional manner, Cam assumed the former. He could relate on some level.

"Cam, I'm hurt," Doc said. "It's like I said—eyes are old hat, nowadays. The market's saturated with optics. It's a buyers' market."

Something occurred to Cam that hadn't before, one of those thought-jolts that likely jerked his more tuned-in audience members out of their seats whenever they came to him. While he'd done his share of simustims over the years, Cam always preferred to be a participant more than a spectator. It may have seemed quixotic for a Looker, but it made sense to Cam—let others see what he was seeing, versus him simply taking in someone else's observations.

"Those are new, right? Not pre-owned?" Cam asked.

"Wow," Doc said. "Yeah. Factory-fresh, not something I plucked from somebody's head in the back. What do you think I am, Cam?"

"Who sold them to you?" Cam asked.

"I don't name names, Striver," Doc said, a perfect finger sliding across his perfect lips. "You're so suspicious."

"I wouldn't be who I was if I wasn't," Cam said, glancing at the gaping Spliff, busy reaching out and touching things that weren't there. "Seeya at midnight, Doc."

NOW & WREN

With time to kill, Cam didn't go far out of the Vision District, wanting to keep an eye on who came and went to Doculus. Cam had found it always paid to pay attention, and so he went to Café Fabulous for a nightcap, managing to stake a booth with a view out a lozenge-shaped armored window that let him keep tabs on Doculus without appearing to.

He nursed the Détente he'd been given by the amphetamine-lanky green-haired server, Wee Tina, who looked at Cam with euphoric crescent eyes, too bright by half. She knew who he was, always treated him well, just in case he was broadcasting. He'd made more than his fair share of acquaintances that way.

"Are you on, Cam?" Tina asked.

"Not at the moment, Tina," Cam said.

She sighed and whirled her way to another client, the moment passed.

For Lookers, it was called Peekaboo—in the rapid-fire world of eyewitnessing, if a Looker went dark, deadpools would spring up, people would wonder what happened to them. Depending how popular a Looker was, the speculation could fuel a kind of panic that would drive up audience engagement.

The art of Peekaboo was not to stay down too long, and to be sure when one popped back up that one was watching and/or doing something worthwhile. Walther Watcher (of *Watcher's Watching* fame/infamy) found that out the hard way when he went dark for two whole weeks because of a stray headware virus only to find when he went live again on an otherwise routine streetwalk that his audience had angrily abandoned him. He'd been stabbed to death by a gang of jilted fans, who (of course) recorded his murder and made a killing from his killing.

Cam toggled his digital clock and saw he'd been down for only a dozen hours. He had plenty of time. His plan was to go live gain with his new eyes, which would dazzle his audience with the clarity and resolution, might get them buying for the higher-echelon packages he provided. The reveal would drive up his audience engagement, and the sharper resolution would pull more in through word-of-mouth.

When Wren and his gang of cops came into Café Fabulous, Cam hoped his timeline would not be messed with. Cops, especially Streetside cops, had a way of doing that. You'd have thought they ran the world, the way they moved through it.

Wren was a massive man, a proverbial slab of vat-grown police brutality who had made detective three years prior and was way too happy to be out of the Shytown PD uniform. Because Cam researched everyone he worked with, he'd dossiered Wren and saw the touchpoints that paved the man's way into law enforcement—a stint in the United National Front Army to assist with the Uforian uprising that led to some hefty modifications to his frame. He'd been halfway blown up by a suicide bomber, but they had put him back together again using classified techniques that left him devoid of a sense of humor. He was otherwise unassailable.

His partners were similarly cybered up—there was Jacquee Nimble, his speed freak, who Cam always liked. She was bright and shiny, Afro-Cuban with a half-shaved head and a peacock blue parted hair wave and propensity for wearing a HUD visor she hardly needed, given the chrome she carried in her. Her reflexes were tuned up to the extent that Cam wondered if the rest of the world looked to be in slow motion to her.

There was grinning Stitch Collins, the man with the stabby hands. He had traded his old hands for these mechanical monstrosities that Cam thought would've earned him the name "Spike" instead, but Stitch claimed that nickname because of his tendency to leave people in need of serious repair after he dealt with them. Slab-tanned and wearing his sandy hair close-cropped, Stitch was one of Wren's most eager enforcers.

Wader Willis was another man-slab, an alabaster imitation of Wren, another former soldier of questionable lineage who was mostly known for being a tough guy of both fearless and fearsome disposition. Cam found Wader's silence deafening and tried to avoid him as much as possible. Wader shaved his head bald and stood out for his cryptic absence of tattoos. Willis was not one to be trifled with, and Cam knew the man would kill him as soon as speak with him.

Of course, the detectives saw Cam. Their optics, like all cop cybereyes, would have been keyed to facial recognition modes that would identify everyone in the room and offer latent targeting pips, if the need arose.

He assumed they were here because he was, and when the other patrons looked over nervously, preparing to be shaken down, Cam could see the look of relief on their faces when Wren and friends turned their attention to him.

"Hey, Cam," Wren said, his voice a deep baritone. He sat across from him, the polyform creaking beneath the man's cybernetic weight, while his face caught the neon shadows. His nose had been broken a time or two in the past and rebuilt from Wren's many appointments with cyberdocs over the years. Plenty of cops spent time in the shops, both from injuries on the job as well as seeking that cutting edge that mattered Streetside.

"Hey, Wren," Cam said. "I thought I was up on my payments."

"Are you on?" Wren asked. Wee Tina spun up, while Wader and Stitch slid in next to Cam, and Nimble paced at the bar. They all ordered canned Ki-Rins, and Tina sped off to fetch them, glancing over her shoulder as she went, thrilled to see that something was up, and that she might bear witness to it.

"No, I'm not on," Cam said. "I'm taking a break."

"Perfect," Wren said. "You get the new eyes, yet?"

"Tonight," Cam said, trying to keep a level gaze with Wren, who was leaning in toward him. Like all cops, the air of intimidation hung like cologne around the man, and it was fatal to show fear before it. Streetsiders knew the capacity to hold one's own with tweaked types mattered. If you folded or buckled under pressure, someone like Wren would simply snap you in half.

"Doc Wellington?" Wren asked.

"Of course," Cam replied.

"We've got a lot riding on it," Wren said. "Audience share, you know?"

"Downslope," Stitch said, drumming his pointy fingers on the table as Tina brought the beers. "You're skating downward, Peeper Creeper."

Wren let his men do their thing, and Cam knew better than to engage with the taunts. Wren liked for them to rough him up verbally a little before he got down to biz.

"For now," Cam said. "It ebbs and flows, rises and falls. Like the sun, moon, and the tides."

"Look at the Midtown poet go, guys. You fall too far, we'll have to recoup our investment," Stitch said. "Wren's put a lot of money into you."

It wasn't actually that way. If anything, it was the other way—they'd dipped their hands into Cam's own profits when it had been clear that he'd become profitable. But Cam wasn't going to bother arguing with the riffraff. Being a Looker meant staying on-target, and the target was Wren.

"What do you need from me, Wren?" Cam asked.

Wren smiled more to himself than to Cam. His teeth were perfect. So often, Streetside hustlers spent scrip on teeth. In the violent work that might be integral to their occupations, a great smile was often a signifier that biz was good.

"We're going to brace some grinders tonight, thought you'd come along, take a look around," Wren said. "Live, of course."

"Real-time, Looker," Stitch said, sneering.

Cam glanced at the timeclock at the corner of his field of vision. There was enough time, provided everything went well. Since he was only getting replacement cyber-eyes and updated software and didn't require a new optical rig, the procedure would be quick, with minimal recovery time. Not like his first time, which had him laid out for a couple of weeks, adjusting to his new eyes, hopped up on pain pills.

"We're talking a raid, right? Not a stakeout?" Cam asked.

Wren's smile extended itself to enfold Cam in its implications. When Wren smiled, things were bound to be broken. Cam had to make sure that he wasn't one of those things. He smiled back at the detective, and for a moment, they both held their expressions before Wren spoke again, his baritone made lower still by his keeping his voice down.

"Naturally," Wren said. "You think I'd bother you with a stakeout? We don't want your fans offing themselves with boredom, Cam."

"Okay," Cam said. "But I have to be back at Doculus before midnight."

"Promise," Wren said, holding up two beefy fingers pointing skyward.

BUMPING & GRINDING

Wren and his crew had piled into an armored police van, one of those grey-toned bulletproof beasts with runflat tires that had a reinforced frame and rollbars within. They rolled through the shiny Shytown streets without a care in the world. Only the potholes seemed inclined to mess with them. But in the hefty van, Cam barely felt them.

Stitch drove, with Wader riding shotgun, both literally and figuratively. Wren and Nimble hung in the back with Cam, and they were putting on their body armor, Nimble handing a vest to Cam as well, which made Wren laugh.

"You're so good to him, Nim," Wren said.

"Wouldn't want anything happening to him that we didn't want to," Nimble said, winking at Cam, who slipped on the vest.

"I appreciate the concern, Nimble," Cam said, relieved to be wearing some body armor at all, inadequate as it was by the standards of what the others were sporting. Their raids were invariably violent, and in this case, the grinders they were targeting were unaffiliated workhorses running some money laundering operation that had not yet been acquired by the local Triads or Yaks. From Wren's perspective, coming down on them now meant a chance for quick scrip that could be rolled into decent profits, provided they were speedy. Once a crew fell under the protection of the big gangs, cops couldn't (or wouldn't) hit them. Such was the order of things in Shytown—nobody operated with impunity.

Wren likened himself to a trideo director. He would actually talk Cam through it, as if he needed to. Cops in Shytown had a sense of theater, and Wren more than most. The man paid attention to optics, both directly and indirectly, which had made his "partnership" with Cam all the more seamless. Whether this was simply Cam talking himself through it or actual reality was something he hadn't fully worked out.

"Now, when I give you the signal, you go live and track the raid," Wren said. "Nimble, you keep tabs on our boy, see to it that nobody pops him. Once we've got control of the scene, you pan across all that scrip. People love the money. I'll say a little something and then that'll be your cue to cut your feed. Leave them wondering. Plus, I don't want anybody watching us divvy up our cut of the scrip. Clear?"

"Absolutely," Cam said. "Not my first raid, Wren."

"Every raid is a first raid," Wren said. "You never know how they'll go down. You just make sure to pay attention and follow our cues."

"Naturally," Cam said.

"ETA three minutes, Boss," Stitch said, eyeing them through the rearview mirror.

"Stitch, you and Wader hop out the moment we're through the barrier. Shoot anyone who resists."

Cam could hear the van revving up as Stitch accelerated, weaving them through the rain-soaked city streets. Because this raid trended in the less overt spheres of law enforcement, they didn't use their flashers or their siren, which required more adroit maneuvering by Stitch as he barreled toward the destination. With limited resources, what Shytown PD concentrated their manpower on the neighborhoods that were worth protecting. Everyone else had to pay dearly for the privilege of police protection.

"Run it, Cam," Wren said, clapping him on the shoulder. Cam mentally toggled the uplink code and his eyes became cameras, tracking all that he was seeing. The old 777s were doing their job, offering steady, reliable POV that was immediately drawing peeps. Cam almost felt a sense of loss that this would be the last run he did with his old eyes, but he quashed that in the face of the adrenal rush of the raid and the anticipation of his new eyes, which would offer even better reception and resolution. He was already dreaming up the things he'd bear witness to, the audience he'd pull in, what he'd charge his audience.

"A minute until impact," Stitch said, over his shoulder. When they were on, Wren's crew all conducted themselves with studious professionalism, wanting to come off sharp on the trideo feeds. Nothing cleaned up a cop quite like a live camera.

"Brace yourself, Cam," Nimble said, patting his arm. Cam clicked himself into one of the seats, while Wren was readying his Tamlier 10mm smart rifle with a 100-round drum magazine. Nimble had her own Fossett .457 magnum nine-shot smart pistol ready, giving Cam another wink when she saw him observing. As the most jacked of Wren's crew, she could afford to engage with something as comparatively slow as the Fossett. In her hands, the big revolver would be fast, accurate, and deadly.

Cam glanced ahead, could see the metal warehouse door coming fast upon them, the black-painted, corrugated metal showing signs of considerable wear and tear, like everything along this part of the River District. It was the site of so much trade, both illicit and permitted. Fortunes were made and lost daily and nightly along its well-traveled paths, with everyone taking their cut if they could get away with it.

"This is it," Stitch said, howling as they brought the van up the loading ramp and right through the metal door. The armored van tore right through it, and they found themselves in the heart of the grinders' operation, striking down an unfortunate goon who had his chest crumpled by the force of the van, tumbling across the room. An expert driver, Stitch swerved the van to the left as he hit the brakes, sideswiping another goon, sending him flying.

"Go! Go! Go!" Wren shouted, throwing open the side door of the van as he jumped out, with Wader hopping out on his side. They slotted targets immediately and started firing, dropping the guards with well-placed shots, while Nimble, playing chaperone, jumped out with Cam, who was keeping his eyes on the action. There was a lot to take in, and his cybereyes were tracking all of it.

Cam understood what was expected of him on this raid. He managed credible pans as he tracked the action. He wanted to put Wren's team in the best-possible light, while also making the grinders feel like a worthy band of outlaws. The art of enhanced observation required Cam to be very present and nonexistent at the same time, and above all, not to flinch as the weapons fired. Cam having suspended his blink reflex to handle all of the noise from the gunfire. Flinching was not welcome, where Lookers were concerned. All reputable Lookers retained their blink reflex to avoid looking creepily mindless in their daily interactions with others. A few freaks went with the staring thing, but they were always tied to specific clienteles that wanted that from their Lookers.

The warehouse was large to the point of being cavernous, with overhead LEDs casting a blue-white light in little islands that ran the length of the place. Above them were suspended metal catwalks that hung, and unmarked, towering columns of boxed merchandise that threw shadows that required Cam to switch to lowlight resolution that flared everything to a feverish green.

Cam could immediately tell that something was wrong. The grinders were there, sure, with their tables and their setup, teams of minders and fat stacks of scrip, but the choice of venue was what triggered Cam.

It was too big.

Nimble saw it, too, her tightly wired reflexes giving her an edge on the rest of Wren's team. They had headware radios, as did Cam, allowing for quick communication.

"Something's wrong, Wren," Nimble said, through the link.

Cam glanced upward, hearing the whir of airborne drones, his eyes seeing a half-dozen of them hovering in the upper reaches of the warehouse, fixed on them. He saw the flare as one of them fired.

"Drones!" Cam yelled, pointing.

The explosive shell had already been fired, the anti-tank round coming at them from one of the drones overhead. It struck Wren full in the chest, detonating, knocking Cam off his feet and causing Nimble to reflexively duck, throwing up her arm.

The drone ordnance blew Wren apart, and Cam saw everything in silhouette—Wren's upper torso and right arm still clutching his Tamlier, the rifle firing off shots as his trigger finger twitched. The rest of Wren had crashed into one of the tables, while Wader, covered in Wren's blood and cybernetic shrapnel, pitched forward, seeking cover, as the drones arced down upon them in a flanking attack.

Stitch speared one of the guards with his clawed hands, only to be struck by a flurry of explosive nanofletchettes that were fired from a blue-bespectacled Mr. Suit who was in the shadows past the terrified grinders scrambling for cover. Mr. Suit was tall and lean, hatchet-faced, with shorn white hair and wearing a black suit. He wore black gloves with the trigger fingers missing. His expression was little more than a hint of a grin.

Mr. Suits were megacorporate bodyguards, with that Streetside term percolating throughout the underworld to identify these typically nameless adversaries who were well-paid to anonymously represent their clients in situations like these. They were almost always elite military, blessed with bleeding-edge cyberware that made them terribly formidable in battle. The degree of megacorp interest and involvement could reliably be gauged by how many Suits were present. One Mr. Suit present meant a corporate finger in the wind, testing which way it was blowing.

His dart gun coughed as the mag-repulse drive system spat the fletchettes into Stitch, who erupted in a cascade of tiny explosions that instantly tenderized him, turning his flesh into bursts of blood and bone and synthelated polycarbonate. The use of a flechette gun indicated that a degree of discretion was expected by whatever client Mr. Suit was representing. Everyone from Midtown and higher liked their peace and quiet, and flechette weaponry was always in vogue there.

Wader roared and fired his Mossington 12-gauge auto shotgun at the buzzing drones, the shotgun blasting apart three of them on the fly, guided by his target tracking system. But Mr. Suit had Wader zeroed as well, and his dart gun perforated Wader with fletchettes that went off like firecrackers across his face, chest, and legs, until he went from corrupt cybercop to hapless man to mangled meat in moments.

Cam saw every bit of this, all of it taking place in nano-seconds, while Nimble grabbed him by the scruff of his neck and yanked him back, firing off her Fossett at the drones and goons, the magnum bellowing with each well-placed shot, dropping three of the grinder guards in half as many seconds, and shattering one of the drones. The other drones—Cam counted six of them—swerved and dove at them, blue-black autotarget-tracking bubbles rotating to attempt to zero in on them. Somebody was driving those drones, someone carefully offscreen, out of harm's way. Nobody set up drone rigs like that without pre-prep, which meant that Wren had stumbled into a trap.

"We are out of here, Cam," Nimble said, as Mr. Suit and the others sought to draw a bead on Nimble, who all but hurled Cam backward with a degree of cybernetic strength far greater than her slender frame appeared to possess. Her speed was incredible, and Cam was grateful for it as she dodged the rain of explosive flechettes that flew from the drones and Mr. Suit, blowing fist-sized holes in the concrete of the warehouse, tracking her as she fled in a ballistic torrent.

Cam tumbled through the warehouse door, into the driving rain, while Nimble darted back, firing carefully, speaking to the Shytown Police Dispatcher on her head-ware radio.

"This is 109, reporting officers down, repeat, officers down," Nimble said. "Mark my position and send Rapid Response Teams to this location. They have drones!"

Whichever drone that fired the anti-tank shell fired again, hitting the van, which detonated with an explosive force that knocked Cam down, and even caused Nimble to take a photogenic speed-dive.

"Kill the feed, Cam. We are getting out of here," Nimble said, collaring Cam, who watched the van burn in the tear in the warehouse door. The drones flitted over the fiery wreck of the van, only to be shot down by Nimble with her Fossett, shattering the camera eyes of the drones in quick succession, blinding them. She speedily reloaded her pistol and shoved Cam away from the warehouse.

Cam's fans were agog at what they'd just seen, judging from the chatter which was scrolling down his HUD, and while Cam was loathe to cut the feed, he knew it would only drive his audience to a fever pitch to leave them on a cliffhanger, so he did, all the while wondering what exactly had just happened, how things could possibly have gone so wrong.

DEAD RECKONING

Cam and Nimble holed up at Cam's place along the river, with Nimble alternately on her headware radio and watching every dark corner. In Shytown, there were endless alleys, angles, nooks, and crannies where opportunities and threats could be lurking.

"What was that all about?" Cam asked, toggling the riot button lock on his apartment door, feeling some reassurance when he heard the maglocks engage. It wasn't great protection but at least ensured that anyone trying to get into his dwelling would have to smash down the door, which might give him enough time to react.

"I don't know," Nimble said, holstering her smartgun. "It was Wren's deal."

He made enough as a Looker to live in Midtown, which meant he had a sliver of space and it wasn't entirely terrible. Nimble cased it anyway, checking the main room and the other. There was even a pretense of a balcony, which she checked as well. Seeing her diligently casing the place made him think back on how things had been for him in Midtown in the wake of the assassination of his parents, of how Finia had looked after him.

His father had made preparations, to his credit. Not everybody did that. But he had. Just like he'd had top trauma team contracts for the three of them, there had been financial coverage for Cam in the event of something untoward and unexpected.

Under the stipulations of the contract, Finia would continue to guard Cam until he turned eighteen. As the assassination had occurred when Cam had turned seventeen, it meant that he had a year with Finia before being on his own.

At the time, the trideo talk about the killing of his parents had rattled assorted media channels. While megacorps fought constantly, rarely was a big one like Yougenix the subject of such a brazen attack. Speculation swirled around who might be responsible, and Cam grilled Finia as much as he was able to.

"Who would do it?" Cam asked, while he paced in the living room, with its mesmerizing view of Downertown, the sea of advertising lights. Even as a young man grieving for his dead parents, Cam's analytical brain parsed what he was staring out at.

Like everywhere, Shytown's advertising regimen broke down into definable categories or channels, geared toward the specific subliminal needs of particular audiences:

SADVERTISING: Ads designed to invoke feelings of wistfulness and longing in viewers.

MADVERTISING: Ads created to provoke strong emotional reactions in viewers, particularly anger.

TRADVERTISING: Ads crafted to soothe viewers with images carefully curated to hearken to more sedate perspectives.

RADVERTISING: Ads made to excite viewers and drive them to hasty action.

GLADVERTISING: Ads formulated to create happy feelings in viewers.

BADVERTISING: Ads forged with minimal audience agency in mind, typically trashy and/or driven toward lines of business where quality took a back seat to the brand promise.

Living in Midtown, Cam mostly saw gladvertisements, tradvertisements, and radvertisements, which kept the prevailing mood relative upbeat, despite the daily troubles and traumas of living in Shytown. For Midtown Strivers, being happy, content, and excited about the possibilities of the future was always preferable to the more fleeting and transactional aspects of city life. Sometimes, when he was feeling down, Cam would look out at the flashing ads that covered buildings and shot into the misty skies and feel better.

"I don't know who did it, Cam," Finia said, standing quietly beside him. She was wearing a grey blazer and a black skirt with black leggings and low-heeled corporate booties with pointy toes that Cam was sure contained retractable blades.

"No idea?" Cam asked. Finia only sighed.

"Your father was popular in Yougenix, and that can earn you enemies and rivals," Finia said. "My contract is to keep you safe, and I'm thinking that finding whoever killed your parents will put you in danger."

Cam didn't like staying in their home after his parents had been killed, but he wasn't in a position to do anything about it until he came of age. Their dwelling was a line that ran along the contours of the building they occupied, like a loft that had been turned on its side and pressed flat against the glass. But it was clean, comfortable, and well-apportioned with holographic art that his mom had collected, and tastefully minimalist furniture that didn't distract from the amazing view.

"No ideas, then?" Cam asked.

"I'm a bodyguard, not a detective," Finia said. "You want to find that stuff out, it's your business, on your own. Frankly, I'd leave it behind if I were you. Your father was well-placed at Yougenix. Whoever offed him had the means to overcome what defenses he'd had in place. That means money. Chit happens, Cam. It's what we say Streetside."

Cam looked at Finia, who hadn't been wearing her shades at that moment. Her black cybereyes seemed to stare through him. It was a look he didn't fully understand until he'd gotten a pair of his own. Her face was as resolute as ever, and as unreadable. Cam thought it had to have been a strange profession, being a bodyguard—having to be innocuous and ever-present, fully-wired, but appearing calm. Was she keeping an eye on threats even then?

"That where you came from? Streetside?" Cam asked.

Finia nodded. "Yep. We all have our trajectories, Cam. For me, my trajectory was Midtown. If your parents had lived, we'd have been in Upperton, maybe watching the planet from the Yougenix Ring, in the Heights. If anybody wanted that trajectory for your family, it was me. Not seeing them fall back earthward that day."

Cam frowned, then laughed bitterly.

"You're not cheering me up, Finia," he said.

"That's not my job, either, Cam," she said.

"I'd just like to know who did it," Cam said, and Finia put a cool hand on his shoulder, giving him a squeeze.

"Let me give you words of advice," Finia said. "Whoever did it, the reasons hardly matter. I know that seems harsh, but Strivers are shallow people. They do things for shallow reasons. For most of them, they do things because they think it'll get them more scrip, more chits. They don't think much beyond that. I haven't been to the Heights, but you're not going to find good people up there, or even great people. You're going to find fortunate people wasting their lives the way they do down here. The only difference is the effects trail after the causes in a way that might seem strange down here in Midtown, or Streetside."

Cam studied the bodyguard a moment, and she looked back at him.

"I don't even know what you're talking about," Cam replied.

"Streetside, everything's about the hustle," Finia said. "We rush around, trying to keep one step ahead of death and dismemberment. In Midtown, the wave frequency is wider between rise and fall. And in the Heights, it's wider still. What might take a split second in Streetside might take generations in the Heights. They operate on different timescales. Odds are good that nobody will ever know why your parents died that day, but if I had to guess, it's that someone in Upperton thought it would give them a few extra points in the markets, which might translate into millions of chits. And so it happened. It's already forgotten."

"Not by me," Cam said. "Not ever."

Finia squeezed his shoulder again.

"Don't waste precious time trying to remember, or, maybe worse, trying to forget," she said. "Just keep your eyes out for the opportunities you can grab."

Opportunities were everything in Shytown. Someone had taken advantage of Wren's own greed and corruption, turned it to their advantage. Watching Nimble smoothly work out that Cam's place was secure made him feel reassured that she wasn't actually part of whatever precisely had gone down.

"Well, somebody else knew about it," Cam said.

"Let me see," Nimble said, flicking her indigo-painted fingernails impatiently.

"I can beam it to you," Cam said.

"No," Nimble said. "I want to see it in your head. *In situ,* dig?"

Cam produced a jackline and put it in at the base of his neck and held the line out to Nimble, who took it and linked.

In that moment, the two of them shared simulated consciousness. Their avatars faced each other across a black and green expanse, Nimble's cranked up nervous system making her avatar sparkle and flicker, while Cam's own more staid self simply glowed. Some jazzed up their avatars, but Cam was pleased to see that Nimble shared a similarly minimalist aesthetic with hers—they simply resembled digital versions of themselves. Plenty of pretenders would zazz up their avatars and try to front that way, whether appearing as gladiators or godlings. Cam found that the ones with nothing to prove with such window-dressing were the most dangerous and emulated that approach.

Not wanting Nimble to go rifling through his head, he went to his filing system and conjured up the most recent recording, a cluster of phosphorescent orange files.

"This one," Cam said, but Nimble was already in it, opening it and filling the digital air around them with rectangles of imagery showing what had happened. Seeing it played that way inside his head made Cam feel strange, like a spectator of his own life. He'd never had someone commandeer his playback like that.

"Who's Mr. Suit?" Nimble asked, zeroing in on the shots of him, which Cam rendered as stills.

"That's what I named him," Cam said. "You know."

Most of the megacorp types never voluntarily ventured below Midtown. To do so either invited robbery and murder or else implied a gangster/government affiliation that might render them the bureaucratic boldness to make such a risky passage. Sending in the Suits made it much easier for the Strivers to keep their hands squeaky clean, or what passed for it in the bizzo world.

"Who was flying the drones?" Nimble asked.

"I didn't see," Cam said. "I'm guessing an ace rigger drone jockey, either on-site or near enough to it to keep overwatch without risking themselves. Although if they were that well-placed, it makes me wonder why they didn't have surveillance on the approach. It's almost like they wanted Wren to make his play."

"Yeah," Nimble said. "A trap's not a trap until it's sprung."

Nimble blazed through his footage, back and forth, and Cam could see Wren, Stitch, and Wader blowing up and coming back together a dozen times before she was satisfied. Having her sleuth within his head made him feel dizzy. He couldn't imagine how Nimble processed so much information so quickly. And he thought that as someone who considered himself a quick study of all that he surveyed.

"You're at least clean in this," Nimble said. "You didn't even know about the run until this evening."

"What about you?" Cam asked. Nimble's avatar looked wounded, frowning flintily at him in pixelated petulance that carried a lot of vibe, enough to make Cam worry that he'd even mentioned it.

"It wasn't me," Nimble said.

"I thought Wren said those grinders were unaffiliated," Cam said.

"They were," Nimble replied.

"They were ready for us," Cam said. "Are we done rifling through my head?"

Nimble copied Cam's footage and filed it in her own head with a breeziness that left him breathless. Rarely did Cam feel so technologically violated and inadequate, made him crave some of the lower top-shelf gear Nimble carried in her.

"Yeah," Nimble said, and she jacked out, her avatar blinking out of digital existence. Cam brought himself back to real time and unjacked. He hadn't had someone in his head since his ex, Merinda, and the memory of that stung a little. The casual intimacy of autonomic association that it brought carried its own weight that hung like a shadow for anyone who'd experienced it. Cam was just grateful he didn't have any brain bruising from Nimble.

"So, now what?" Cam asked.

Nimble was processing her options. He'd never spent this much time in her company and watching her jacked neurosystem work gave him fits. She just kept moving, like she couldn't keep still. Anyone who flew that way paid a price for it eventually, if they didn't simply cyber up and replace flagging wetware with ever-cooler chrome. Nimble ran hot, and that took a toll.

"The RRTs didn't find any bodies," Nimble said. "They're all gone."

"Ghouls?" Cam asked.

"Maybe, but I think whoever was backing the grinders took advantage and harvested Wren and the others. They had a lot of gear. Even combat-damaged, there's scrap and salvage that could be sold."

Cam wanted to be of assistance to Nimble, but only to get her out of his hair sooner. He didn't like having a detective at his apartment. As a Looker, he just assumed everyone was snooping on everyone else. Detectives were at the bottom of the pyramid of power, which put them head-and-shoulders above Lookers like himself. There were many layers to the stratosphere, and detectives knew their way into those places, the avenues in the direction of real power. Cam was purely an onlooker, not a participant. But Nimble could have a future if she was quick enough.

"That's your angle," Cam said. "You track the meat markets and see who's coming along selling spare parts. I mean, Wren and the others had to be serialized, right?"

Nimble's eyes flitted as she was thinking about something.

"Yeah, natch," Nimble said, dialing them up in her head. "PD always tracks that. Dispatch, this is 109. Have tracers run on fallen officer wetware. I believe someone's harvested them."

"Copy that, 109," the Dispatcher said. "What's your current location?"

"Best not say," Nimble said, glancing at Cam. "I'm going to lay low until I have a better sense of what's going on. Believe there may have been a breach somewhere. 109 out."

Cam hadn't been privy to her call, but Nimble had verbalized it, so he could at least hear what she'd been saying, which he decided was for his benefit.

His own headphone went off. It was Moxie Monocle, his agent. Moxie was Midtown flash, prone to Asiatic styles of dress with purple and blue tresses that flowed like gel upon her well-coiffed head. She wore a monocle that was a HUD and uplink interface, an intentional archaism that was a result of her owning her own squeamishness about getting her eyes done.

"Cam!" Moxie said, her voice all lipstick tinsel in his head. "I saw your feed, it's all over the trideo! What happened? Are you alright?"

"Fine, Mox," Cam said, watching Nimble raid his fridge for some metabolic kicks. Anybody that jacked had to keep the calorie count high. She found some SoNoodles Cam had gotten the other day and helped herself to them. She ate with precision, the black chopsticks she'd found clacking out a beat with each bite.

"Fine-fine? Are those your new eyes? They look the same to me," Moxie said.

"No," Cam said. "I'm getting them at midnight."

"Whew," Moxie said. "I was worried you'd been ripped off. Along with maybe getting shot. Still, good trendlines on your coverage. People are talking."

"That's good, I guess," Cam said. He worked his way past Nimble and snagged a Tengu Beer from his fridge. "What do they think happened?"

"Betrayal, obvi," Moxie said. "Dirty cops. That sort of thing. They think maybe it was Nimble."

Cam glanced at Nimble, grateful that it was his headphone, and that she didn't appear to be tapping him. Nimble had finished the noodles and was spearing some soy-cubes with the chopsticks and dipping them in Metasoy she'd found in his fridge. Her voracity was offset by her implacable manner, making it seem like the most natural thing in the world as she systematically worked her way through his food.

"Yeah, I can see that," Cam said. "Except she got me out of there. If she was in on it, maybe I'd have been dead, too."

"Good point," Moxie said.

"What about Mr. Suit?" Cam asked.

Moxie frowned fetchingly. Nobody in Shytown frowned more photogenically than Moxie. Cam wasn't entirely convinced that it wasn't part of her marketing tools.

"Nobody knows who that guy is," Moxie said. "No facial pattern recognition on file, although with the Eyeconics, you'd have had better resolution, would have probably nailed it."

"Coulda Woulda Shoulda," Cam said. "Didn't. Well, I'm sure the Peepers will be all over that. Just topline me any pet theories that have legs."

"Of course, Cam," Moxie said. "Are you otherwise okay?"

"Right as acid rain," Cam said.

"You call me as soon as you get your new eyes," Moxie said. "You know how I worry. Who's minding you while you're recovering?"

"Probably Detective Nimble," Cam said. "Feels like she's halfway moved in already."

"Hmm, if that doesn't work out, don't hesitate to call me, Cam," Moxie said.

"Of course, Mox," Cam said. "Who do they think bumped off the cops?"

"Audience majority thinks maybe the Triads," Moxie said. "Or Russian *Bratva*. Nobody thinks it was the Yaks. Just not their style."

Cam could see arguments on all sides, with crystal clarity—the brutality of the hit was certainly in the Russian wheelhouse, but the capricious nature of it could have been Triad, too.

"There's also a small segment that thinks maybe it was you, Cam," Moxie said, grimacing.

"Me? I didn't even know about the gig until tonight," Cam said.

"I'm just reporting what people think," Moxie said. "Staging a hit to boost your ratings, you know, that kind of scene."

"I'm no copkiller," Cam said, glancing at Nimble, who'd finished her noshing and was rooting around for her own Tengu. "I had a deal with Wren."

Moxie nodded, smiling awkwardly.

"You know how people are, Cam," Moxie said. "When are you going on next?"

"After I get my new eyes," Cam said. "ETA around a dozen hours, is my guess."

"Okay," Moxie said. "Talk to you then."

Cam hung up, seeing Nimble watching him while she drank her beer. In the dimmed light of his place, with only the gladvertisement glare rising and falling, she looked enigmatically elegant, shrinkwrapped in brand promise and sultry shadows.

"It wasn't me," Nimble said.

"Oh, so you *were* tapping me?" Cam asked, irritated.

Nimble grinned at him, shrugging her shoulders. Her grin betrayed nothing while revealing everything, most especially her perfect teeth that felt out of place with a member of the police. Maybe it was for on-the-spot photo opportunities or earned her points with higher-ups. Good teeth were quick-and-dirty status symbols in the world. Cam suspected they were likely weaponized, too, and envisioned Nimble biting her way out of imprisonment if she had to.

"I'm always tapped in," Nimble said. Cam sat on his gunmetal blue sofa, while Nimble paced. Outside, it rained, and the city lights flared in the dark. His place had minimal décor, since it wasn't so much a home as a hideout, and Cam never kept anything there he wasn't willing to abandon in moments.

"Okay, so who do you think did it?" Cam asked.

"I'm not at liberty to say," Nimble said, taking another swig of beer.

"Any suspects?" Cam asked.

"It's an open investigation," Nimble said. She wasn't going to give him a thing. It felt even more cop-like as she drank his beer and ate his food.

"So, are you my roomie, now?" Cam asked.

Nimble smirked at him over her Tengu. Her worldly smirk enticed at least as much as it offended Cam's sense of propriety. She was his guest as much as he was her prisoner.

"As I see it, your deal with Wren now flows to me," Nimble said. "Last woman standing. Besides, like Moxie said, you need someone to look after you after you get your eyes done."

Cam studied her, trying to see the line where sarcasm ended, and sincerity began. With Nimble, it was always hard to tell. Her jangly way was difficult to break down. Her motivations were as murky as they were multifaceted. Even her angles had angles.

"Do we have a deal, Cam?" Nimble asked, shooting out a hand for him to shake.

"Fine, fine," Cam said, shaking her hand. She gave him just a hint of a squeeze, so he could feel just how strong she really was. Cam held onto his smirk for dear life, feeling the coolness of her chromed hand seep into him.

DEADEYE

idnight came quickly, and Cam and Nimble made their way to Doculus without incident, relying on the Midtown Pedway to get them there before they took the Streetside plunge. Cam hadn't had a bodyguard since Finia and felt a bit of confidence in having Nimble beside him, as people got out of their way. The Pedway was how many navigated Shytown, relying on the elevation and prevalence of corporate Pedcams to keep travelers relatively secure by Shytown standards.

The Pedways had been built decades ago when there'd been a demand for Midtowners to not have to walk the streets anymore, when they still had enough pull to get those kinds of projects undertaken. For the megacorporations, it was a way of building consumer thoroughfares that were somewhat safer than Streetside.

It wasn't that the Pedways were really that much safer than the streets; rather, the flight or two or steps upward to reach the Pedway meant that only the more motivated and/or desperate criminals ventured up there. If hooligoons (as they were known) harassed you on the Pedway, it meant that they were far more inclined to do you harm than the average random street rats. It was a risk vs. reward sort of dynamic.

The periodic Pedway Police Drones couldn't be everywhere at once, and the criminal elements who populated the Pedway treated the PPDs as a navigation hazard more than deterrents. However, Pedway PD officers were not averse to throwing a perp off the Pedway if they stepped out of line and labelling it a suicide. Unofficially, they referred to it as an "eviction" when it took place, with the understanding that walking the Pedway was a privilege, not a right. Given how efficient the Ghouls were about body recovery, it didn't disrupt the everyday life of Shytown residents much, unless they happened to be walking under a Pedway when such an eviction occurred.

"They all know you're trouble," Cam said. "It flows off you."

"Good," Nimble said. "Makes my job easier."

The Yaks had historically safeguarded sections of Midtown, but they were in decline in Shytown and elsewhere, leaving the Triads to fill the void. Triads were, by their nature, wilder in spirit, which made the Pedway more festive than it otherwise needed to be. Travelers upon the Pedway could find themselves in as much danger from the Triads as from other gangs.

"Maybe it was Oniyaki who bumped off Wren," Cam said to Nimble by way of his headware radio.

"Please," Nimble said. "If you're going to play in my head and name names, at least use code, Cam. In case anyone's listening."

"I'm just saying," Cam said, watching some Stiffs strolling to Drinky's Bar with some bodyguards, trying to look comfortable in their reflective rain ponchos over their company suits. If they were anybody, they wouldn't be walking. Enough money to rent some bodyguards, but not so much to travel in style. Their shadows danced against the city light reflected on the slick streets, with badvertisements vying for their attention at every step.

"You leave that to me," Nimble said. "The speculating part."

"As I see it, whoever tipped Wren off to the score was in on it," Cam said. "That's who you lean on."

Nimble gave Cam a sidelong leer, which he couldn't entirely process as to its meaning. In Shytown, the smile of a cop could mean anything.

"I know, Cam," Nimble said. "You a detective, now?"

"Every Looker's a sleuth," Cam said. "We look at absolutely everything."

Nobody understood how it went with Eyewitnesses. Everything was worth looking over, sooner or later. Meaning could be found in the simplest of things.

They reached one of the Streetside stairs that led to the Vision District, marked by some holoprints of blinking eyes that seemed to look at them as they approached. Some of them winked, others stared, all of them blinked in an eerie approximation of life. Cam considered Doc's ads to be a mix of radvertising and gladvertising, to put prospective patrons in the right frame of mind. The colors were bright and welcoming, creating emotional responsive pathways that Doc could work to his advantage.

Cam peered over the Pedway railing, gazing down at the rain-soaked street awash in the neon glow of everything. Cars, trucks, bikes, and people hustled their way. Even at midnight, Shytown was full of activity. Nobody ever stood still in Shytown, unless they were dead.

"We're here," Cam said. "I really appreciate this."

Nimble flicked ahead of him, reaching the first landing.

"Don't get all emotional on me, Cam," Nimble said. "Let's just get to Doc's."

Cam trotted down the steps, alert for anything out of place. The Pedway stairs were mixes of ancient concrete and rusty steel that somehow managed to endure over their long lifespan, betraying scars of erosion all across them in monochromatic streaks and cracks in the concrete. Once built and long-forgotten, they remained for everyone in Shytown. Some of the choice Pedway stairs even held toll-keepers. They were low-level street goons who timed their presence on the stairs between PPD flights and the timely appearance of Triads or Yaks. Anyone who failed to pay them was most commonly evicted. Luckily, there were no tollkeepers on this set.

"Do you think they were targeting me?" Cam asked.

Nimble shrugged, zipping down to the next level. Cam admired the way Nimble moved, that predatory blend of lithe lethality and functional formality.

"Maybe, Cam," Nimble said. "Can't rule it out."

"What and who *can* we rule out?"

Nimble laughed, watching some walkers ascending the stairs—they were a young couple, looked like tweak-ers judging from their rain-soaked clothes and absence of breath masks and similarly ring-eyed hunger in their bloodshot eyes. Nimble let her hand rest on her Fossett, as if she even needed to. They could see how wired she was, knew that if they tried anything, she'd perforate them before they even finished starting.

They passed her and eyed Cam, who hastened to stay near enough to Nimble to imply an association. Cam hat-ed the Squiffs, because one never knew quite how it'd go with them. He'd seen Squiffs throw themselves over walls, light themselves up against defense grids, knife people be-tween dumpster dives for a chance at some scrip without a thought about the consequences.

Before he'd traded his eyes, Cam worried that he'd be at risk of becoming a Squiff. Living Streetside always posed that risk, which was why he avoided it. He and Moxie had made an arrangement where either one would off the other before they slipped down that route. It wasn't so much a suicide pact as mutually assured euthanasia. Thoughts like that took him back to his not-so-distant past, when Finia had been guarding him full-time.

Cam took Finia's advice literally when he'd turned eighteen, cashing in what he could get away with selling, starting with his childhood Upper Midtown home. The scrip that came from that sale went to him getting someplace cheaper, Lower Midtown, and with trading his eyes for a cybereye rig. He'd been shopping for the right starter rig, and Finia had noticed, before he'd taken the steps he'd taken.

"Are you serious?" she asked, while he pored through the trideo radvertisements featuring the various ocular rig brands he might consider. The radverts made everything look promising, and it was easy to get caught up in the vivid vibe they threw off.

"Yeah, well," Cam said. "*You* have them."

She half-smiled at him, but only barely. Finia's half-smiles carried a gravitic weight to them, never to be taken lightly.

"And look where that got me, Cam," she said. "You have pretty eyes. Baby blues. You seriously want to trade them for some off-the-shelf rig? To do what? Become a Looker?"

"Yep," Cam said. "I need to *see*. To really see what's going on. I need to see more than my parents did."

"Now you're just being cheeky," Finia said. "If you stick with your schooling, there's a place for you at Yougenix. Your mom and dad burned a route for you there, Cam. You'd be stupid to trade it for running Streetside. You belong up here. Find yourself some antiseptic corporate chickie here and become a power couple like your parents were. There are plenty of them here. You do *not* want to go downstairs, Cam. Trust me on that score."

But as much as his parents had been marketed as a power couple at Yougenix, all Cam could see was them blowing up in the sky, struck down by their unknown assassins. He didn't like the feel of that sort of life. For all of the work they'd done, it had vanished in moments, because someone waved a finger or made a headphone call. They'd never seen it coming, for all of their corporate powergaming.

"You're lucky," Finia said. "This is a comfortable place, Cam. You could do something here. This place is swank. You'd squander that for what? Becoming a Looker?"

It wasn't something he could explain to her. Finia impressed him—her cool professionalism, her low-key killer persona, while never tested in his eyes, was something he aspired toward. His parents had been proper Strivers, meteoric, whereas Finia was something else. Always there, always ready. He didn't know how her life might play out but was confident that she'd land on her feet.

"Maybe I want to honor my mom," Cam said.

"We both know you're not that sentimental," Finia said. "Lookers are true hustlers and runners across the Grid, Cam. They're desperate for attention. They'll do absolutely anything to get noticed. Up here, you can relax, at least for now."

"I still have to earn," Cam said.

"And Yougenix would take you, with your pedigree? You're halfway through the door," Finia said. "We could wrangle an extension on my bodyguarding contract—I could be your driver, your chaperone, your confidante. Whatever you needed me to be."

The casual way she put that out there, the cool tones of her voice, it conjured images in his head, this Upper Midtown meta-life he might have with Finia and the ghosts of his parents for company. Finia was ten years older than he was—still young, but wise in the ways of the world. There was comfort there. And yet, he didn't want to be under her wing.

Whatever you needed me to be.

The idea of it was too tempting. Finia had that hyper-fit build of the artfully chromed, a sort of caricature of humanity, like a living mannequin, slim and sleek, but so strong. He'd been on his share of dates with Midtown girls, and was certain that Finia could teach him plenty of things he had yet to fully understand.

"No," Cam said. "Better a clean break once your contract's up. You've been the best, Fin. You're the closest thing I have to family anymore. And maybe that's why I have to let you go."

"Stupid," Finia said. "Stubborn. Like your mother. Relentless, like your father. If you'd been brewed in a beaker, they couldn't have brewed a better version of themselves in you. We could be happy here. Really close to it, anyway. Content, even."

It was funny to hear a bodyguard talk about contentment. Just like Streetside grit infected a person, maybe Midtown comfort did that, too. Softened a person to the point where it was all they'd know or want to know. Fearful of risking it, losing it, yet desperate enough to do whatever it took to retain it.

"Come on, now," Cam said, while she stared at him, hand on her hip. She was beautiful in the most utilitarian of ways that he found difficult to define. Sharp lines, nothing wasted.

"Streetside will devour you, Cam," Finia said. "Down there, you're just so much meat. That's *all* you are to the people down there, the street rats. The Ghouls will grind you up. There's nothing but death in Downertown. A sweet boy like you will be destroyed by it."

"Still guarding my body," Cam said. "Right to the last minute."

"It's a good body," Finia said. "Shame to waste it."

When her contract was up, her birthday present to him was a long hug goodbye, and a stroke of his cheek with a coolly chromed finger. He never saw her again, not in person.

Years later, when he'd started to gain traction as a Looker, he'd seen that Finia had taken an Upperton gig for Yougenix, guarding some biotech whiz who'd made a name for herself with some game-changing gene-editing technology. He'd glimpsed her in a trideo feed about the researcher migrating to the Heights, Finia in her wake, shadowing her, the way she'd walked with him, her shades hiding her eyes. He'd felt both happiness for her and a lost sense of longing for the security she provided.

"Well-played, Fin," Cam said, feeling more wistful than he thought he would, gazing up at the stars on a rare cloud-free night, his cybereyes giving him killer resolution, watching the near-orbit stars of the Heights shining as they hurtled in their orbits.

The memory of it almost dragged Cam's eyes skyward, but the clouds were thick and there was nothing to see but the reflections of radvertisements and gladvertisements in the air, the marketing messages billowing and distorted by the tempestuous clouds spitting hard rain down on them.

"Come on, Looker," Nimble said. "Get your pretty head out of the clouds, Bizzo."

As Cam joined her, Nimble watched them perhaps closer than she had to. Then they went the final patch of stairs to the street. Only assers and idiots cluelessly walked Shytown's streets at midnight by themselves, or else bizzers out to close some keen deal that had to be settled ASAP. Either scenario put them at greater risk, depending on who was around. Whether in a herd or a pack, it paid to travel Streetside in numbers this late.

"You should dock Doc for having this go down now," Nimble said.

"Let's just get to Doculus," Cam said. He didn't have to point it out because they both knew where it was. Doc's criminality was offset by his dependability, and his customers more often than not found that they valued both in equal measure.

They went to the front of his place and Cam fingered the intercom. He was mindful of the shadows around them. Some drones flitted overhead, going wherever they were going in the rain, their buzzing high-pitched, distinctive, but noncommittal as they sped off without so much as glancing at them.

"Doc, it's Cam," he said. "I'm here for my appointment."

He could see the autogun and camera within tracking them. The maglocks opened and in they went, Cam first, Nimble behind, minding the door until it locked behind them.

Doc was visibly dismayed by the presence of the detective, his exemplary lips pursed in disapproval, his eyes raking over Nimble, coldly assessing her.

"What's this, Cam? Your bodyguard?" Doc asked.

Nimble smiled at him, those perfect teeth that likely cost her a fortune in payoffs and bribes bright in the artificial light.

"That's right, Doc," Nimble said. "You have his eyes?"

Doc produced the box he'd shown Cam earlier.

"The very ones," Doc said.

"Let me see them," Nimble said, all cop-voiced, expecting compliance. Doc flipped open the case, and Nimble ogled the eyes that stared up at her. "They'd better not be counterfeits."

Doc looked mortally wounded, stifling a gasp.

"Detective, please," Doc said. "I have my reputation to consider."

"That you do," Nimble said. "Get to it."

Doc's picture-perfect features petulantly pinched as he regarded the detective, only to switch to something more desperately benevolent when turning his attention to Cam.

"Shall we proceed, Cam?" Doc asked. "In back, obviously. You stay up there, Detective."

"Of course," Nimble said, taking a seat in Kiosk Two, reversing the monoform chair so she could lean on it while keeping her attention on Wellington, who ushered Cam behind his plastic curtain and pointed to his seat.

Despite his Streetside location, Doc kept his workspace surprisingly clean. His logic was that with eyes, even artificial ones, cleanliness mattered. He used a passive static room filter that kept particulates at bay, as well as an internal filtration system to manage the smoggy days. Fortunately, in the rainy season in Shytown, dust and smog were less common, although the mists and fogs could present challenges.

"Nothing here you haven't seen before, Cam," Doc said, waiting for Cam to take off his leather jacket, which he tossed onto a nearby chair. "Although I must say that bringing a member of the constabulary here was very louche of you."

"Louche?" Cam asked, toggling his dyslexicon for the definition, which flashed into his field of view.

Louche /looSH/ *adjective* 1. Disreputable or sordid in a rakish or appealing way.

"Terribly," Doc said.

"I do like to keep you on your toes, Doc," Cam said. "I am rakish that way."

"That you are, Cam. Your Omnitrac Ocular Housing System can accommodate this upgrade," Doc said. "Thanks to my foresight, one might say. We're really talking about a simple ocular swap versus a full buildout."

"Makes me wonder why I had to go to all of this trouble for a midnight switch at all, Doc," Cam said, laying back on the white-cushioned operating table. The filtered air had the peppery tang of antimicrobials. Cam thought maybe it was some point of professional pride for the man, the astringent scent of antiseptic wall washes conveying comfort in some manner.

"What about headware memory? All of that?" Cam asked.

"You have enough to handle the Eyeconics, Cam," Doc said. "You knew that. Are you testing me?"

Seeing Doc standing there with his ocular extractor in his hand like it was a weapon made Cam smirk. The first extraction was the worst, the obligatory organic panic at the loss of something integrally interconnected in one's natural body. Once a person had cyberoptics implanted, it was a comparatively straightforward procedure, devoid of pain beyond the momentary discomfort of signal loss.

"I wouldn't dream of it, Doc," Cam said, laying back. Doc dimmed the lights in the room and toggled something, which put a pair of red laser crosses on the ceiling.

Sirens sounded somewhere outside, but nobody at Doc's place paid them any attention beyond the mute acceptance of their existence. If Nimble wasn't worried about it, Cam wouldn't be, either.

"Eyes locked on the crosses, Cam," Doc said.

"I remember, Doc," Cam said.

"Don't waver, blink, or twitch," Doc said, pushing a button on the extractor, which caused it to click into its ready position, the padded spiderlike limbs splaying outward in a circle. "And please tell me you're not on, Cam."

"Not on," Cam said. "I don't do reruns, Doc."

Wellington scoffed, having remembered that Cam had done a live feed extraction when he'd first gotten the 777s, which had terrified his audience and served as a major voyeuristic draw among the fans once word got out about Cam running a live eyeswap. None of the other reputable Lookers had thought to do that, although it was rumored that some of the snuffamatrix people had blazed those particular trails decades before, with markedly bloodier results.

The last time Cam bothered to look into it, there were an estimated five thousand Lookers in the country, and maybe two million worldwide. The numbers varied because Lookers were always coming and going, many of them getting killed, many more getting their fancy eyes stolen by organ grinders. The market for organs (real and artificial) was always thriving, and a nice set of cybereyes was particularly valued, despite Doc's complaints about eyes being less often traded. The truth was that they had migrated to the secondary organ market. Someone coming in the way Cam did was relatively novel. But that's how Cam was, preferring to go and do what other Lookers didn't do.

"Alright," Doc said, settling the extractor into position. Cam held his gaze on the crosses on the ceiling over Doc's shoulder, feeling the padded extractor limbs settling around his eye. Activating another button prompted some of the limbs to hold his eyelids open, while the central extraction arm, equipped with a high-tension suction pad darted out, slapping onto the 777 and drawing it forth with an almost comical popping and clicking sound.

Doc carefully pivoted, depositing the 777 into a crucible containing blue sanitizing fluid.

"Halfway there, Cam," Doc said.

"One-quarter, Doc," Cam said.

Cam hated going dark most of all. For him, it was the worst part of the procedure. For a Looker to be unable to see was a fate worse than death. He was completely at the mercy of Doc, and in Shytown, this was anathema.

Doc worked quickly, and the extractor plucked out his other eye, and Cam was now functionally blind, with only Doc's calming voice for reassurance. It took him back to when he'd first traded away his eyes, with Moxie being there with him, having talked him into getting the procedure to begin with. She'd brought it up in her tiny apartment in Greater Streetside. They'd been in bed after a long night at Slinky's, one of the more active Midtown-adjacent nightclubs, where Moxie worked as a hostess and Cam half-assed it as a cardchecker, making sure everyone paid up their tabs, sending in actual bouncers when people came up short. They'd crossed paths after he'd sold his parents' place, was still shopping around for the right pair of cybereyes, the perfect rig, not letting anybody know where he'd come from, lest that come back to haunt him.

"You really should become a Looker, Cam," she said.

"Yeah? Why?" Cam asked, not telling her how much he'd been thinking about it.

She smiled at him, laying on his shoulder, tracing his profile with a fingertip.

"Because you'd actually do it," Moxie said. "I know I wouldn't. One of us has to do something."

Cam laughed, the two of them in the dark while outside, Streetside, somebody was getting shot: *blam-blam, blam, blam.* Moxie flinched with each shot, while Cam didn't. Gunshots never affected him. Maybe he'd heard them too many times growing up. The memory of the murder of his parents had left scars that never fully healed.

"You're a flincher, that's why," Cam said.

"Yeah, okay," Moxie said. "I'm squeamish."

Cam kissed her forehead, tasting the alkaline-metallic hint of fresh sweat and old makeup. Moxie's voice was as beautiful as she was, a sultry sing-song that could disarm all but the most tone-deaf of Spliffs.

"Yeah, you are," Cam said.

"I'll be your agent," she said, kissing his shoulder. "People *like* you, Cam. And you see everything. You always notice everything."

"I thought you hated that," Cam said.

Blam blam. Blam. Blam.

"Properly channeled, it's golden," Moxie said.

"I see," Cam said.

"You will," Moxie replied, kissing him while more shots fired. They kissed while bullets whizzed by unseen, for people and places unknown.

"I'm going to just clean your OOHS," Doc said. "Although you've done a good job maintaining it, Cam. The eyewash is going to be lukewarm, as you no doubt remember. Just stay where you are for now."

Cam rather liked the eyewash part of the swap, as it felt almost spa-like. For a street doc, Wellington had a gentle touch. Some street docs were hasty, but Doc Wellington took his time with his patients, and Cam appreciated that.

"Why do you stay Streetside, Doc?" Cam said. "Seems like you could do better in Midtown. Maybe even Upperton."

"I'm fine where I am. Things get complicated when you move up. Clients get demanding and they expect more from you. Down here, people are just glad to see you," Doc said. "Eyewash is commencing in three, two, one..."

He poured the eyewash into Cam's eye sockets, and Cam could feel it bubbling, the sound carrying to his ears and within his head. The warmth of it was soothing, and Cam dared to relax a moment, the first time in days.

"Turn your head to your left, Cam," Doc said, and Cam did as he was instructed, the eyewash flowing out. "You're going to like the Eyeconics. They're very smooth. Minimal wear-and-tear on the OOHS."

"Great to hear," Cam said, as Doc fiddled with what Cam assumed were the Eyeconics.

"Alright, Cam," Doc said. "New eyes coming in. Lay back and lie still."

Cam did was he was told, and Doc placed the 360s smoothly and with precision, and Cam felt relieved to have them in place. His OOHs accepted them with a quick click, and Cam could feel them moving smoothly in the ocular orbits.

"Okay," Doc said. "Now, here's the video uplink jack."

Doc tapped Cam's left hand and put the jackwire in it. Cam took it and slipped it to the nape of his neck, where his pair of links were. He popped the cap off one and slotted it.

"The uplink will take a few minutes, but you should be able to see once it's online," Doc said. "I'll set the clock."

"Is it done?" Nimble asked. Cam hadn't heard her approach.

"Yes, Detective," Doc said, irritation apparent in his voice. He didn't like being monitored. "Once the uplink occurs, he should be good to go. And just to prepare you, Cam, I'll need the second half of my payment once we've confirmed that they're working properly."

"Of course, Doc," Cam said. "I'm good for it, you know this."

"Just a formality, I'm sure," Doc said.

"What'll you do with the old ones?" Nimble asked.

"Resale," Doc said. "I'll clean and wipe them, blank them and they'll find a home somewhere, I'm certain."

"Gross," Nimble said.

"Oh, please," Doc said. "You're about the last one in the world who'd be twitchy about this kind of thing, judging from all the bodywork you've had done. Who did your eyes, Detective? Not me, that's for sure."

"Nobody you'd know. Still gross," Nimble said. "I wouldn't want somebody's hand-me-down eyes."

"You'd be surprised," Doc said. "There's a thriving re-sale market. Cam's always been a great client, takes very good care of his merch. The nice thing about the 360s is they practically take care of themselves. Top shelf. Anything greater would be milspec, not remotely street legal."

Nimble chuckled at this.

"What more can they do?" Nimble asked. "They're only eyes."

Doc looked put out by that, his displeasure straining his artfully sculpted features.

"You'd be surprised what one can do with the right set of eyes," Doc said.

"No, I wouldn't," Nimble replied.

"Uplink complete," said a computer voice just as Doc's timer went off. "Initiating Eyeconic Ocular Protocol."

Cam saw a moment of static in both eyes before they came online, and he actually let out a gasp at how crisp the resolution was. He could see Doc and Nimble like he'd never seen them before, in high-res splendor. They both looked fantastic, making Cam feel like he'd been missing out on everything he had only thought he'd seen before.

"Wow," Cam said. "These are incredible, Doc."

Doc smiled at this, reached for his digital ophthalmoscope, which he slid into place over Cam's new eyes. The scan went quickly, and all indicators came up green. He then took out a stylus with an LED light on it and had Cam track it with both eyes, and with each individual eye, moving it around and holding it, letting him note its position, confirming alignment. Doc moved that stylus like a wizard with a wand, each word of affirmation like a conjuration. After a few minutes of checking this, Doc was satisfied.

"They're working fine, Cam," Doc said. "Now, if you can just get me the remaining payment, we'll be on our way."

Cam, still jacked, accessed the remaining funds, and beamed the chits to Doc's covert bizzer account. Doc noted it and smiled, while Nimble, already bored, flitted to the front room.

"Pleasure doing biz with you, Cam, as always," Doc said. "And remember: don't forget to blink now and then."

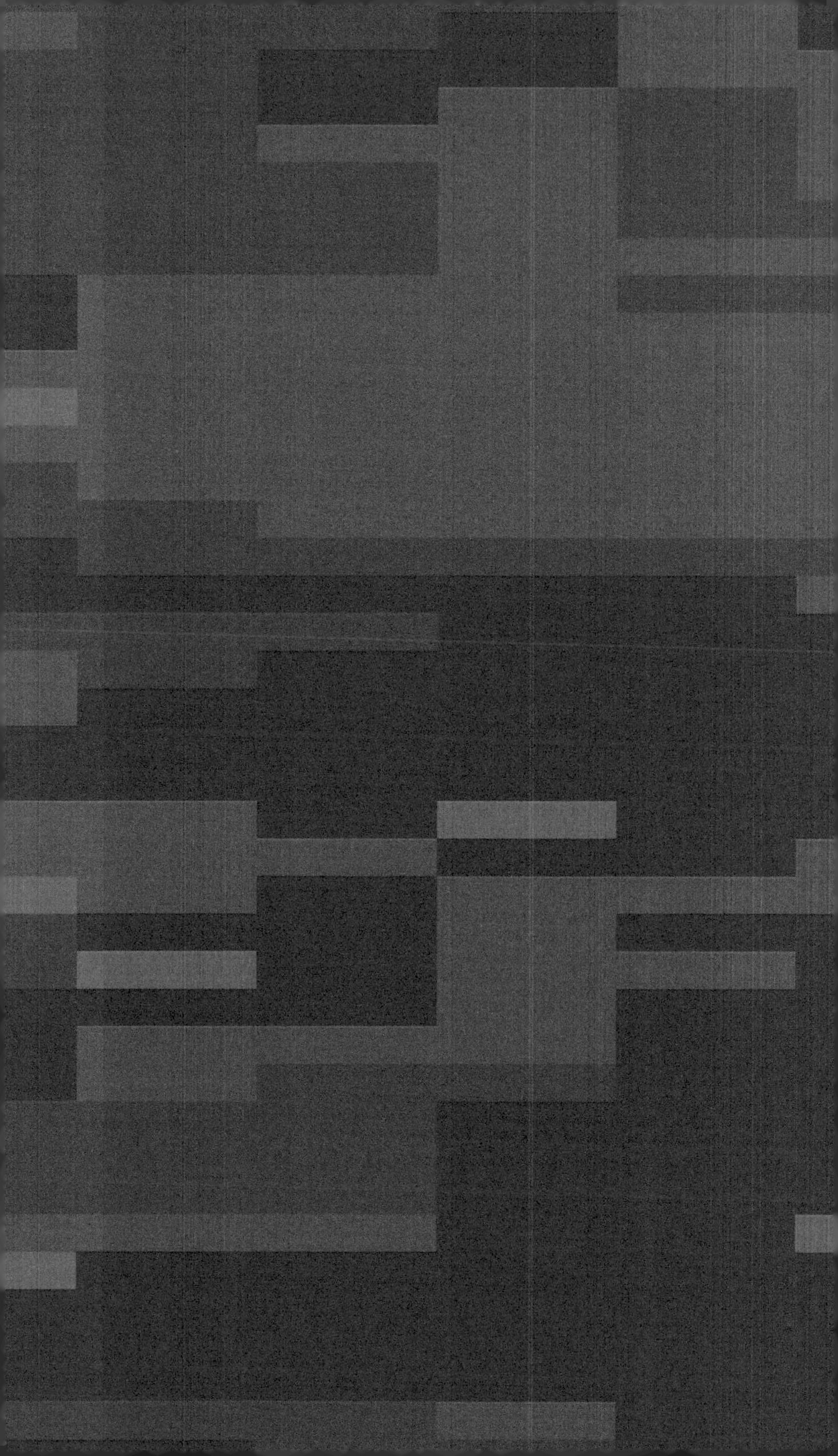

VANTAGE POINTLESS SLAUGHTER

Nimble left Cam on the Pedway, while he reveled in his new eyes before he went live with his feed. He had his own personal tests he liked to conduct with a new set, which included focusing in on distant objects, zooming in, cycling through the various modes. The new cybereyes were fantastic. Worth every chit he'd thrown at them.

The rain had cleared for the moment, leaving the city breathless and foggy, the smell of ozone and oxides lending a certain aroma to Shytown that wasn't entirely unpleasant for those used to it.

"Don't film me," Nimble said. "Better I lay low since what happened. I'm going to do some investigating."

"Shouldn't I go with you?" Cam asked.

She shook her head slowly, as if finding the question laughable, despite not laughing. The look in her own cybereyes said it all.

"Policework, Cam," Nimble said. He didn't understand, since he'd accompanied Wren and his crew on any number of outings over the years. He felt like he had a handle on the work they did.

"I know how that's done," Cam said. "Maybe I could help."

"Not with *this* kind of policework," Nimble said. "Look, you just do your thing. Enjoy your new eyes. Give your audience something to look at. I'll be doing what I do to find out what I can. I'll find you when I need you."

"What about our deal?" Cam asked.

"This *is* part of the deal," Nimble said.

And with that, she was gone, zipping away in her jacked-up, quick-walking manner, and Cam felt very alone along the Pedway, so he went live, knowing some fans would be notified when he reconnected. The hardcore Peepers and Creepers always had notifications triggered so they could jump onto his feed straightaway.

"Hey, all, Cam here," he said. "With my new eyes, as you can see."

He panned around, flicking through some of the view options, to the delight of his insomniac audience. Everything was better with the new eyes, and he was even more certain it was the best money he'd ever spent.

Damn, Cam!

I see! You see! We see!

Way cray! All the way!

So crash, Cam!

Cam walked past a number of Midtown bars and clubs, the neon flashing and enticing in the light, while still more fog tried to roll in after a momentary stop in the rain, breaking up the gladvertising lancing skyward. He cycled through the various modes, which fired up his audience, who savored the sneak peeks.

He saw some Pedwarriors watching him, one of the lower echelon gangs, prone to red track suits and white sneakers and shaved heads, with the women keeping bangs and long locks on either sides of their faces, while the guys going closely shaved. Their racket was mainly mugging. They saw Cam and started after him, while

Cam recorded, trying to move across one of the Pedway lattices to reach a way around them, ideally toward one of the PPD security drones.

"Pedwarriors," Cam said. "Damn Nim for ditching me. This might get ugly."

His onlookers were in favor of him shooting the Peds, and Cam did carry a Glock 91 smartgun, but he didn't draw it, preferring to evade at the moment.

Shoot those Peds, Cam!

For realz. Gun'em down, yo!

Click-Click-BLAM, Cam!

The Peds had fanned out, three of them on his tail, while the other three were fast-walking across one of the other catwalks to try to cut him off. They didn't look chromed, which made them more desperate and dangerous, since they'd see him as an easy target for robbery.

"Yeah, they're after me, alright," Cam said.

The Peds were four men and two women, and all of them were zeroed in on Cam, and all of them looked hungry as they fished out aluminum baseball bats which they banged on the Pedway railing, the metallic clangs marking their passage. The aluminum was likely scavved and reforged by some Streetside salvage smelters, who were often tied to the local gangs in a reciprocal arrangement— the gangsters would rob Streetsiders and bring loot back to smelters, who'd salvage what they could and melt things down, allowing for a form of laundering to take place. Salvage ingots of various metals were traded briskly Streetside. That this crew were brandishing those bats meant that they were doing alright.

"Enough, already," Cam said, pulling out his G91 which he held aloft so they could see it. "Let's test out the autotargeting optics on this, shall we?"

He was pleased to see he had all six of the Peds targeted as they approached, having now cut him off on his route, so that Cam was effectively stuck on a catwalk with Peds on either side. The new eyes were carefully tracking their distance to him, targeting reticles offering him kill shots if he pulled the trigger.

"Hey, Swanker," the leader said. He was a young man with an orange-dyed fuzzhead, buggy eyes and a wide, toothy mouth. "You must be some kind of badass to walk out here this late all alone. Or a dumbass."

"That's Cam Sexton, Griever," one of the women said. She had electric blue forelocks and bangs and face tats of black lightning bolts arcing all over her face, angling toward her eyes, or away from them, depending on one's perspective. "He's the trideo guy. A Looker."

"Griever" acknowledged that with a sidelong look. Cam ran a scan of Griever, saw his street alias align with his image, identifying him, to the delight of his audience.

Griever's a retriever, Cam. Watch out!

Sticky fingers!

"That a fact?" he said. "You a trideo man, Looker?"

"That's me," Cam said. "My show's *Sightseer.*"

"Never seen it," Griever said. "You on right now, Looker?"

"As a matter of fact, I am," Cam said. He put his back to the Pedway railing, mindful of the Peds trying to outflank him. His G91 had twenty-five rounds, which was more than enough to deal with this group, but if they rushed him, it would be bad, even with the targeting.

"Like right now? Peepers watching?" Griever asked.

"Right now," Cam said. His HUD was ablaze with fans watching this go down. Bets were being made over whether Cam would be merely mugged and robbed or murdered. Cam thought the Peds looked like tweakers, having the amphetamine edge to them which made them twitchy Squiffs.

"So, you've got eyes on us," Griever said. "For now. Pricey eyes."

"Nobody's taking my eyes," Cam said. "Least of all, any of you."

"Tough talk from a Looker," Griever said. "See, my bet is we can rush you before you get any shots off."

Cam leveled the G91 on Griever. When in doubt, always target the mouthy ones, at least when dealing with streetpunks. He was the alpha of this little pack.

"Try me," Cam said. "This could be your big break, Griever."

The autotargeting HUD had them luminous in red outlines. Cam didn't have a full tactical array, unfortunately. That would have allowed for proper autotargeting, where his shots would be guided stepwise through his target allocations, greatly increasing the accuracy. It would be up to him to successfully aim and shoot. But his HUD did allow for a pip that showed whether or not he was on the mark, which considerably boosted his chances of hitting.

"Leave him alone," came a voice from behind them. Cam instinctively flitted his eyes toward the source of the voice, his HUD using his contacts repository to identify the person as Abby Normal. It wasn't her real name, but she'd used that street name for so long that it's all anyone ever knew her as.

Abby was a Yak enforcer unlike any other. She was petite and wore her hair in a dark shag, with a propensity for wearing outfits of black and grey. Her face was oval, with big eyes and a little nose. She wasn't wired the way so many were, but rather, was the product of something else entirely—she was bioengineered from birth in some secret Yak labs to be strong, fast, and tough. Her enhancements were natural, which was particularly fancy. Only those with scrip to burn had access to biomodification like that.

The Peds turned and looked at her. Griever, in particular, was displeased at the sight of her. A Yak bioenforcer was less than welcome on the Pedway, being as out of place as a nano-ninja. The practitioners of nanojitsu were strictly Upperton-fancy, mostly confined to urban legends and wild stories of all-but-invisible assassins operating clandestinely. Someone like Abby was equally alien to Streetside and Midtown living.

"Hey, we weren't doing nothing," Griever said. "We're Triads, anyway. You can't touch us, Yakker."

Abby was terminally stoic in bearing, but the presumption of Griever teased out the faintest of smiles from her. While the Yaks and Triads weren't anywhere close to chummy, there was a degree of professional pride both ancient orders possessed, and it was absurd to think that these Peds would be meaningfully associated with the Triads.

"I don't think you are," Abby said. She produced a katana from over her shoulder, giving them a taste of her speed, which Cam was happy he'd captured, as it dazzled his audience. One moment she had open hands, the next moment, she'd drawn her sword.

Samurai lady crazy to bring a sword to a bat fight.

Crazy like a foxwoman, Dog.

I almost know what that means, yo.

She nano-ninja, Spliffs.

Not so.

Kensei the word, maybe.

Stop yakking cray.

Cam knew a Yak katana wasn't some museum piece or poxy trinket. Rather, it was a heavily engineered thing, made from purest alloyed steel and no doubt protected from the elements with some high-flex paradiamond poly-coats that made it even stronger.

Cam thought Abby had the right read of it—the Triads were always scooping up new recruits, but he doubted they'd bother with Pedway trash like this. Standards were standards, even when it came to hooligoons.

"We are, Yak," Griever said. His attitude was a rarity—while the Yaks didn't have nearly as much pull as they had in decades past, they still were not ones to be crossed. Leastways an organic assassin of theirs like Abby was.

"Enough, already," Cam said. "Walk this off, Peds."

The other Peds looked at Griever for guidance, and Griever was holding his ground, either through ego, arrogance, desperation, or all of the above.

"Damn stupid, walking around with a katana, is what I'm saying," Griever said.

"Better than a bat," Abby replied.

"Is it, though?" Griever asked, and he and his buddies made the mistake of rushing Abby. Cam caught all of it, his hypermindful cybereyes tracking it.

Abby moved in a blur, blocking Griever's wild swing, slashing him across his stomach with the katana, splitting it wide open in a splash of blood that dropped him to the Pedway with a strangled gasp. Then she struck out again, the blade catching another of the Peds between his neck and shoulder, which took the fight right out of him, along with a lot of blood. The third Ped swung hard for Abby, but found only air and Pedway railing, as she'd moved effortlessly out of his way before countering with a scalp-slicing cut that poured blood into the Pedwarrior's eyes.

The other Peds, seeing Griever and the others dropped so quickly, took off running back the way they'd come, their sneakers squeaking on the ground as they fled.

Abby looked at the wailing and wounded others, giving the head-wounded one a kick in the midsection to take the wind out of him. Griever was curled up in a ball on the Pedway, clutching his stomach, while the one with the neck wound had sat down, his face pale as he tried to staunch the flow of his own blood.

"Looker," Abby said. "With me."

She flicked her katana, splashing blood on the fallen, taking out a grey cloth with which she wiped down her sword in one smooth motion. She then sheathed the blade and motioned for Cam to follow as she pocketed the handkerchief. Her movements were catlike, devoid of insecurity, doubt, and pretense.

Cam followed, making sure to pan and capture the wounded Peds in great detail as he moved through them.

"Oh, and go offline," Abby said. "Like now."

Cam knew better than to disagree.

THE YAKKETY YAK

Abby had taken Cam to a flying limousine, a sleek black beauty that was waiting for them just past the portion of the Pedway where they had been. He and Abby were the only passengers in the back, and Cam hadn't seen the driver as they whisked up and away.

Flying cars were a hallmark of the past, since few could afford them. As such, only the wealthiest and/or most brash sorts of Strivers made use of them. They were a semi-obsolete novelty these days, calling back to a more plebian past where simple displays of tech like that made an impression. Nowadays, the wealthy didn't even have to put on airs; they were simply rarely seen this far down. Cam supposed that what Yaks remained were forced to straddle the worlds, and their traditionalism kept some things in use, like the flying cars. The limo ride was smooth, the antigrav providing envy-inducing transit unavailable to most everyone.

The interior of the limousine was low-key luxurious—black leather seating, a minimalist-fancy wooden table in the center, and dim blue neon lighting strips. There was a bar at the far end, and Cam felt like getting a drink, but didn't want to push it with Abby.

Cam really wanted to record it, but as Abby sat across from him with her katana across her lap, he didn't think she'd be amenable to it. Still, one of the things a Looker lived with was going where others didn't, so he went there:

"Mind if I, you know, capture this?" Cam asked. "I've never been in a flying limo before."

"I told you to go offline. You *know* I mind," Abby said. She held out something in her hand, a black rectangle with a pair of prongs on it. "Put in this Stopper."

"Oh, come on, now," Cam said. Stoppers were datajack plugs that blocked data processing such as video uplinks. "That's just rude."

"I insist," Abby said. "You don't like it, you can always step out."

She nodded to the door as the limo climbed, Shytown swirling below, the cityscape a disorienting pile of needle-like buildings and radvertisements shooting up into the sky in luminous banners depicting gloriously unattainable things like offworld colonial investment opportunities and orbital transgressions in the Heights.

"Where are we going?" Cam asked.

"You know where," Abby said. "Stopper first, then we talk. I could install it on you myself, if you'd prefer."

Cam snatched it up and jacked it, not wanting to give the Yak enforcer the excuse to overpower him. Not that he'd necessarily mind Abby laying hands on him, but under the circumstances, it would be too clinical for his liking.

His internal headware monitored the intrusion, which barred his video uplink.

"There'd better not be any viruses in that thing," Cam said.

"It's clean, *Gaijin*," Abby said. "Boss wanted me to be discreet, so I'm being discreet."

Cam wondered why she was being like this. He'd worked with and for Oniyaki for years since he'd become a Looker. He knew Abby wasn't fond of him, wondered if she was doing this just to rattle him before meeting with her boss.

"I don't think a flying limo is particularly discreet," Cam said.

Abby walked over to the bar, took out a pair of cut crystal glasses, put cubes of ice into them and then poured whiskey into both, before walking them back. She set Cam's glass on the table in front of him.

"Drink up," Abby said, holding out her glass for him to clink. Cam doubted it was drugged, under the circumstances, so he followed suit, watching her sip her drink before taking a drink of his own. It was heavenly whiskey.

"What does Oniyaki want with me?" Cam asked.

"He just wants to talk to you," Abby said.

Down on the street, it was easy to forget that stuff like this existed above the fog, smog, and cloud layers. Upperton—or Lower Upperton, as Cam thought of it, since the Heights was where the real action was—could be seen as a world unto itself. Nobody in Lower Upperton ever bothered to think about what went on below them anymore than people living in the Heights concerned themselves with whatever was happening planetside. Cam wondered how colonists felt on the extraplanetary outposts, what they thought of Earth. As much as he thought about it, colonists were split between desperate workers taking advantage of opportunities to greedy elites who wanted to stake their claims offworld, far from the theoretical oversight that they resented on the planet.

"Okay," Cam said. "Seems a bit much."

"He wants discretion," Abby said.

"He has that," Cam said.

"I suppose he wants more," Abby said. "You'll know soon enough, Gaijin."

"You know, I don't think I can be a Gaijin in my own country, Abs," Cam said.

"It's not *your* country anymore," Abby said. "If it ever was."

Cam's mind was working—that they'd used a Stopper meant that whatever Oniyaki was going to talk about, he didn't want any chance of Cam recording any of it. That meant it was something white-hot. Typically, that meant something worth plenty of scrip. Whether that meant scrip for Cam or Oniyaki was another matter. Or, more directly, it was a matter of how much Cam might get, relative to Oniyaki.

Lookers who were any good had to be at least reasonably sharp. As Cam saw it, some of them—and he included himself among them—were great detectives. Seeing clearly required it, both in terms of career advancement and survival.

He triggered his thermographic optics and could see that besides Abby and the driver, they were alone in the limo. The Yaks were always about keeping things minimal. Or maybe Abby was simply more than enough for the task at hand.

Cam studied her through the thermovision, watched her cool frame function, devoid of any ware whatsoever. The Yak tendency toward organics rendered them rarities in the wider world. There was purity in tradition for them, he imagined. He saw it as a disadvantage, relative to other gangs. Triads loved hardware, headware, wetware, cybernetic enhancements. They gloried in it. And the Russian *Bratvas* were shameless about their own mods, adopting a bizarre kind of chromed bravado where the bigger and badder the mods, the more they wanted everyone to know about them. The Yaks were models of restraint by comparison.

The cultural mythos around them was that they didn't use modifications because they didn't need them.

And that made him think he knew what Oniyaki was up to. He decided to go there, if only to bother Abby.

"Oniyaki commissioned the hit on Wren," Cam said.

Abby took a drink before replying, the ice clinking in her glass as she studied him a moment.

"I don't know anything about it," Abby said. Thermograph showed her as cool as ever, no spike in temperature. She was a practiced liar.

"Has to be that," Cam said. "Only reason he'd Stopper me."

"We're almost there," Abby said. "You can ask him yourself."

"I intend to," Cam said, finishing his drink. He switched back to normal eyeview and feigned nonchalance, while Abby took the moment they had to get a few zings in.

"I don't know what he sees in you," Abby said.

Cam smiled at her—the cockiest, most mocking smile he could manage—which passed for Looker bravado. She was unfazed.

"What do you mean? I'm charming," Cam said. He could see the neon pillars of the sky-high-rises around them, Lower Upperton proper. The places where people could pretend there was nothing below them even as they lived lives where nothing was beneath them.

"If you say so," Abby said.

Abby was, of course, immune to his charm. She always had been. Her work and his work didn't play well together—she didn't want to be seen, and he wanted to see everything. A Yakuza assassin didn't want publicity. Even the glimpses of her he'd gotten on the Pedway would be enough to feed his audience's rampant voyeurism. He could imagine people cross-referencing datafiles and identifying Abby Normal, who was known without being especially famous.

By that logic, her street persona worked exactly as intended, drawing attention away from the true her, whoever that actually was. It made a strange sort of sense.

"Why haven't we ever, you know..." Cam let that trail.

"You're not my type, Cam," Abby said. "And you know that, too."

Cam enjoyed provoking the assassin. It wasn't great sport, but it was suitably distracting to entertain him. While she was serenely terrifying, Cam always did his best not to give in to that emotion. While he'd never know the truth of it, he fantasized that it might earn him a shred of respect.

"We're here," Abby said, as the limo slid smoothly into its berth. Cam could see out the tinted windows as they went from the clouds to the well-lit interior of the launch bay. "Finish your drink."

"Already did," Cam said, rattling the cubes in the glass. She slipped the glass from his hand with a perfect sort of motion borne of enhanced biological speed and experience, setting the glasses aside as the limo door was opened by a Yak goon, who waited for Cam and Abby to step out. Abby motioned for Cam to go first, so he did, stepping out into the cool air.

In Lower Upperton, the air was rarefied, and the winds always blew. Cam shivered in the chill, seeing at least a dozen autogun turrets trained on him—red-eyed spheres with guns of every variety. Cam could only imagine someone attempting to raid this place. While Lower Upperton had its share of megacorporate intrigues, they seldom involved shootouts.

"This way," Abby said, as she and the goon—who was himself a black-suited block of youthful brutality—walked Cam through some secure doors that scanned him.

Abby sighed, smoothly snatching his G91 before he could protest.

"I almost forgot," Abby said, handing it off to the goon. "Don't worry, Cam. You'll get it back. Oh, and shoes."

She toyed with him, too, it seemed, pointing to a little alcove where an attendant in a tan uniform waited. He was a young man who bowed politely and accepted the shoes, giving them each a pair of sand-colored slippers they put on.

Once they cleared the security entry, the inner doors opened and Abby led Cam inside, leaving the other goon behind. Within the security perimeter, Oniyaki's palace was quite lovely, being a feast of fountains and actual bonsai trees, of black, gold, and red lacquered paint and wall hangings depicting mountains, waves, and dragons. There were statues of demons and lions in gold and scarlet, staring ferociously at them. The air smelled clean, with a hint of unfamiliar spices and willful citrus.

"What now?" Cam asked.

Abby led him past polished and patterned pine floors to some screens that were slid open by additional Yakuza, all young men whose faces registered nothing Cam could discern beyond a tireless sense of duty and adherence to protocol and decorum. He resisted the urge to scope the place fully with his new eyes and knew that the Stopper would prevent him from even photographing any of this.

He always thought it was curious that Abby, a woman, was so prominently represented within Oniyaki's operation, since the Yaks were hyper-masculine in their traditions and their organization. The use of her had to have been some form of psychological torment on the part of

Oniyaki, who enjoyed playing those sorts of games with friends and rivals alike.

"Hey, Abby, are you a freelancer?" Cam asked. Abby glanced at him, her face unreadable.

"Why do you ask?" Abby said.

"Because no Yak would have a woman involved in what they do," Cam said. "It's just *not* done. I've always wondered."

"Wonder away, Cam," Abby said. "Oniyaki keeps me on retainer. If I were to speculate, I think he enjoys the existential threat I present—that rivals inclined to cross him might end up killed by a woman, which can be seen in some quarters as a fate worse than death. The dishonor would be mountainous."

"Wow," Cam said.

Abby offered up the barest whisper of a smile, something Cam wished he could have captured for posterity. As it was, he'd simply have to remember it.

"And he pays well," Abby said.

"You ever think of taking on other clients?" Cam asked.

The trace of a smile remained, the ghost of bemusement.

"Like you, Cam?" Abby asked.

"For example, yes," Cam said.

"You couldn't afford me," Abby said. "And, no, I don't. When you work for Oniyaki, that's a lifetime appointment, however long that lifetime is."

"Ah," Cam said.

"You'll understand that more after you've talked to him," Abby said. "If you don't understand that already, Gaijin."

They found themselves in a room with three unadorned black futons within it, and a low, lacquered wooden table of glossy black and red. Hanging from the walls were monitor screens, and at the center futon was Oniyaki, who stood and bowed when Cam and Abby entered. Cam and Abby both bowed. Cam hadn't had a sitdown with Oniyaki in over a year.

Oniyaki was a young Yak, even pretty in the rough strokes of the brush that built him: lean, sharp-chinned, his black hair wantonly long, almost touching his shoulders, as if he didn't have to answer to anyone. Which, at least in Shytown, he didn't.

He wore red shirts with black suits and black ties like he didn't have to care. Somewhere on him he carried a kubotan. Cam knew that because it would come out from time to time, like a magic trick. He knew when it appeared that somebody was going to get hurt. Oniyaki never smiled when he did this; he just did it.

"Did you get the eyes, Cam?" Oniyaki asked.

"I did," Cam said. "The new ones."

Oniyaki gestured for Cam to sit, which he did, taking one of the flanking futons, while Oniyaki took the center one. Abby walked to one of the walls, sliding open the screen, revealing a small cooking station, which included a traditional teapot and cups. She began the preparation of the matcha.

"Good, good," Oniyaki said. "Any problems?"

"Not with the eyes," Cam said. "They're just right."

Oniyaki nodded, while Abby went about making the tea as if she wasn't hearing every word. There was a certain bravado in Oniyaki having his favored assassin brew his tea for him. Whether it was trust or cockiness, only Oniyaki truly knew.

"Good, Cam," Oniyaki said. "I see you so often at the Plastic Fantastic. I watch you. Always looking."

"I like to see," Cam said. The Plastic Fantastic was one of the best Midtown nightclubs, and Cam frequented it when chasing biz, as there were always people worth seeing there, things worth seeing. Plus, as a well-run club, it hopped in all the right ways. Anybody who was looking for somebody visited it.

"How much?" he asked. "How much do you see? Do you want to see more?"

"Badly," Cam said. Abby brought over the tea on a little wooden tray, placing the cups in front of Oniyaki and Cam before standing to one side, over Cam's shoulder. He glanced at Abby, who didn't look at him, while Oniyaki watched. She bowed, and he accepted it with a nod.

"I thought so," Oniyaki said. "Which is why I cleared your schedule for you."

Cam felt himself go cold.

"Wren?" Cam asked.

Oniyaki only smiled, sipping his tea.

"You like your job, Cam?" Oniyaki asked. Engaging with him was part of Oniyaki's game, almost challenging him with his casual, courteous manner. Oniyaki was many things, and being polite was one of them, even when he was being terrible.

"Of course I do," Cam said, taking his own drink of tea. The matcha tasted of seasonings Cam had never known outside of Yak meetings—bright, spicy flavors that could offer him no memories beyond his time in the company of the Yaks, like cardamom, orange peel, and coriander.

"Of course you do," Oniyaki said, scrutinizing him. "I like you, Cam. You are both intrusive and discreet, flexible and unwavering. I value that discretion and am amused by your willingness to intrude, to go where you are not wanted. I respect your unwavering commitment to your profession, and your flexibility in the application of it."

An ask was coming. He greatly resented the Stopper, as he found he depended on his eyes and their ability to record what he was seeing, didn't like having to keep track of things with his own unaugmented brain. Attention spans and historical memory were so very last century.

"I try to chase down the stories worth observing," Cam said.

"Yes," Oniyaki said. "Precisely so. You Lookers are part spies, part diplomats, part journalists, part entertainers. You make origami in reverse, taking the world as you see it, the elegant constructions people build around themselves, and, finding the folds and seams in the lives of those you observe, you pull them apart carefully, revealing them to be only colored paper, after all."

"Poetic observation," Cam said, sipping his tea to buy some time and hopefully sense what Oniyaki was wanting.

Oniyaki picked up a remote and brought the wall screens to life, showing Sandra Scene and Victor Glimpse, their feeds. Sandra was at an Upperton debutante ball, mixing it up with heiresses and autocrats in what looked to be an orbital outing at the Penderton Spindle, while Victor was detailing a megacorp acquisition where Gaiacon was buying up Deltaware Transnational, surrounded by elective surgical-perfect Stiffs gladhanding one another before the escorts came in.

"I don't like their feeds," Oniyaki said. He flicked to some other feeds, lesser Lookers who Cam either didn't know and/or didn't worry about—"care" was too strong a word. Thousands of other Lookers all trying to find something worth sharing with the watchful world. Some of the feeds showed darkweb content—torture porn, snuffwork, home invasion, stalking, that kind of thing. There were Lookers for that as well, operating below Streetside level, definitively underground, always enmeshed in organized crime in some fashion. Cam hoped that wasn't what Oniyaki had in mind for him.

"I don't watch that stuff," Cam said. "Nothing to see that someone, somewhere, hasn't seen before."

Oniyaki smiled at him, drank his tea. Abby glided from her spot to pour some more tea for them both, before slipping ghostlike back to her spot.

"You are wrong, Cam," Oniyaki said. "There is much to see, if you know where to Look."

He hit his remote again and the wall screen behind him showed a split screen between Sandra Scene and Victor Glimpse, both of them cosmetic-modded to look as synthetically beautiful as they could be, like a couple of living dolls. Cam was young enough to view that with contempt, confident that he'd never turn himself into one of those mod-mannequins. He told himself that as a Looker, his point of view was the most important thing he offered, and his looks were merely accessories to the larger effort.

Suddenly, something happened to their feeds. Cam noticed it right away, seeing a masked figure appear in both of their feeds at the same time, a figure in an all-black business suit, wearing a Chinese demon mask—red-faced, snarling, three-eyed, wearing a crown of little skulls. And the figures detonated simultaneously, killing both of their feeds.

"Wait, what?" Cam asked, as Oniyaki clicked through the trideo, showing panic and chaos at the two gatherings. "What happened, there?"

"A terrible tragedy," Oniyaki said, watching the audiences of Glimpse and Scene obsess over stills and trideo clips of the mysterious assailants, around six million onlookers. "Looks like terrorists."

Security footage at the events showed the detonations from a distance, the force of the explosions jarring the surveillance cameras. More clips rolled in as people jockeyed for the best representation of the explosions. Cam imagined that's how it went when his parents were killed. People always flooded crime scenes when they could, in hopes of securing clicks, chits, and notice.

"How?" Cam asked. "Security for those events would have to have been ultratight. Where were their bodyguards in all of this?"

"There's always a way," Oniyaki said. "You just have to know where to look."

Cam made the connection.

"You framed the Triads," Cam said. "Yes?"

Oniyaki shrugged amiably.

"Did I?" he said.

The footage showed a breach at the Penderton Spindle, quickly sealed before any heiresses could be sucked out into space. Diamond Class MedEvac RRTs were on the scene in a heartbeat in both locations, while private security and even government authorities were blocking off the crime scenes. It was happening too fast.

"What did you do? Suicide bombers?" Cam asked.

"I didn't do anything, Cam," Oniyaki.

He raised his cup of tea in praise of Cam, who raised his own cup uncomfortably. Oniyaki had made it look like some mad Triads had assassinated the top two Looker draws in a coordinated attack. Cam wondered who those masked bombers were, whether they were Yaks, androids, or something else entirely. Were they volunteers and/or fanatics?

"You're now the Number One Looker, now. Congratulations, Cam," Oniyaki said.

"Just like that?" Cam asked, watching the coverage swarm. If not for the Stopper, he'd have looked it up himself, would've been in on the feed. Its absence bothered him.

"Just like that," Oniyaki said.

Cam's few years working in Oniyaki's orbit told him that there was an unspoken expectation here. He glanced at Abby, who was only standing there, acting like she wasn't aware of all of it.

"And now what?" Cam asked.

"A new show," Oniyaki said. "A new feed. Your term, yes? Someone like yourself, maybe. Right now, I'm calling it *Lookout.*"

"*Lookout?*"

Oniyaki nodded. He flipped his remote again and the screen behind him produced some additional, smaller screens.

Looking at the screens, Cam knew they were darkweb, full-blown black market hatchet job feeds that pervs and psychos paid scrip and chits to peer into the eyes of the lunatics who ran those types of feeds.

"I don't do darkweb," Cam said.

"No, you don't," Oniyaki said. "But darkweb's gonna do *you*, Cam."

The Yak boss smiled coolly at Cam. He half-thought of bolting but knew Abby would stop him before he got three steps away. And as high up as they were, there was no place to go but down.

"I don't understand," Cam said.

"*Lookout* is a new stimsense show," Oniyaki said. "Someone's going after you. To be sporting, I'm going to tell you who. You have seventy-two hours to survive. You survive, you win. You get some money sent to one of your accounts. The secret ones. You lose, you die. Badly."

"What?"

"All you have to do is survive," Oniyaki said. "You know how to do that. You're a survivor, Cam. It's what I like about you."

The smaller screens just hovered there, depicting dark-web horrors—interrogations, torture, sniper assassinations, bloodsport brawls, sexwork, sex offenses.

"I'm not a killer," Cam said.

"No, I know that," Oniyaki said. He gestured for Abby, who walked over and snapped a metal collar around Cam's neck. It beeped when it clicked, the cool metal giving him chills. He yanked at it, but it wasn't coming off.

"What's this?" Cam asked.

Oniyaki smiled, while Abby looked on without expression.

"Darkweb bondage toy," Oniyaki said. "Thrall collar."

A little digital number clock appeared in the upper righthand corner of the big screen, with 72:00:00 on it. The countdown clock appeared in the corner of his new eyes, too.

Cam's other hand went to his neck, and he tugged at the metal collar with both hands. But it was locked tight.

"Careful, Cam," Oniyaki said. "That collar comes off before the timer's up and it explodes. Like those Triads you saw onscreen. Big explosion. Enough to blow your head clean off."

Cam felt sickened by this. The metal collar was warming against his skin.

"You just need to stay alive until that timer runs out," Oniyaki said. "You do that, you win the first episode of *Lookout.*"

"First episode," Cam said. "This isn't funny, Oniyaki. I have my own show. What am I supposed to tell my fans?"

"You tell them nothing," he said. "Certainly nothing about me. You be creative. And if you did say *anything* about me on your feed, I'll detonate it directly."

He pointed to a black rectangular box with a red button on it, sitting on the low table, just within Oniyaki's reach. The button was a big one, hard to miss.

"Make things up," Oniyaki said. "Make something up. Say you just woke up with it."

"People saw Abby show up," Cam said. "They might suspect."

"They might," Oniyaki said. "You divert them."

Cam's head was racing, he was trying to figure out what he needed to do.

"Who's after me?" Cam asked.

"Stabbo the Cyberclown," Oniyaki said, and one of the screens showed Stabbo slashing a victim with his razornails, his white gloves bloody. The POV camerawork made him look particularly ghastly—this white-faced apparition with blood all over him.

"Stabbo?" Cam asked. His reputation was dark and dismal. A former augmented soldier who'd fought in Fragistan and Cyanistan, he'd gone rogue at some point, running his own darkweb stimshow (*"Stabbo's Meatmarket"*). Stabbo ran a feed primarily focused on kill-or-be-killed urban assassination and torture, chasing down digital desperados. His milspec modifications consisted of adaptive camouflage, razorfingers, augmented strength and speed, and a host of other gear. "Stabbo's out of my league. I mean, the man's a serious killer."

"He's insane," Oniyaki said. "But not out of his mind. We approached him with the show idea for *Lookout* and he was interested. All of those augments he has cost a lot to maintain."

"Oniyaki, I've been good for you," Cam said. "I always get your share to you, don't I?"

"Yes, very admirable," Oniyaki said. "Reliable, even. Exactly why I chose you. That, and you're so street smart."

"What do I get if I win?" Cam asked.

"Money, like I said," Oniyaki said. "More audience. All those clicks. People will be fixated on your story. And if you manage to kill Stabbo, you get him as salvage. That's all yours to keep. I imagine he's worth a lot with all those mods."

The other screens went away, and there was Stabbo, seeming to grin at him through the screen, white-faced, orange-haired, blue-eyed. He looked as artificial as he was, like he reveled in it.

"Does he know?" Cam asked. "Did you put a thrall collar on *him?*"

"No, just you," Oniyaki said. "I'm paying him to hunt you down. Three days. Ground rules are clear—he must kill you with his hands. No shooting. No sniping from a distance. Up close. Personal. Intimate, even."

"Oh, thanks," Cam said. He could only imagine what was in Oniyaki's head. By eliminating Sandra and Victor, it would raise Cam's profile. Which would raise the incremental-yet-aggregated profits he'd make from viewership. Something sensational like a lunatic such as Stabbo tracking him down would draw viewers. That growth in viewership would mean hefty revenue for Oniyaki. "What will the audience know?"

Oniyaki was beside himself with pleasure at the prospect of his scheme.

"That's the best part," Oniyaki said. "Stabbo's been talking about it for the past week, how he's going to kill a Looker. He doesn't know who, yet. I reached out to him through intermediaries. He's aware of the rules and expectations. He gets generously funded if he finds and kills the target within seventy-two hours. If he fails to make that deadline, then he gets nothing."

"If I survive, what then?" Cam asked. "I'm not doing another episode."

Oniyaki smiled at him.

"I will honor that," Oniyaki said. "Only one episode. I just need you to sell *Lookout* for me, to help it get a big draw. It should help me propel the show forward."

"What are *my* rules?" Cam asked.

"You don't tell anyone about me," Oniyaki said. "Especially not the authorities. Most important. You can do whatever you need to do in order to try to survive those seventy-two hours. Only there's a built-in tracker on the collar. Stabbo will know where you are, to within five hundred meters."

"That's not fair," Cam said. "He doesn't even have to hunt me."

"He'll have to hunt once he's within five hundred meters," Oniyaki said. "Audience participation will skyrocket. People will be monitoring your feed and his to find out what's going on. Oh, and that's another thing. You must have your feed on nonstop for the next seventy-two hours. No peek-a-boo."

Cam's head was swimming. He'd have to hire a bodyguard. That much was very clear. Someone to protect him. And maybe he'd lock himself into a vault for the duration of *Lookout*. That was a possibility. Of course, if Stabbo gained access to the vault, that could get ugly for Cam. It wasn't in his nature to hunker down. He'd stay mobile. That was the only way.

"When does it start?" Cam asked. He felt absurd asking these sorts of questions of Oniyaki.

"You'll know," Oniyaki said. "Once the Stopper's taken off, it starts."

"Starts with the Stopper," Cam said. "Ironic."

"Isn't it?"

Oniyaki steepled his fingers in front of him, watching Cam.

"How do I know you won't just blow me up the way you blew up Sandra and Victor?" Cam asked. "Or Wren and his guys, for that matter?"

The Yakuza boss looked almost entertained by the suggestion.

"They were in my way, Cam," Oniyaki said. "You're not in my way. We're friends."

"Like hell we are," Cam said, tapping the thrall collar. "This isn't something a friend would do."

Oniyaki laughed, glanced at Abby, who stepped forward, which made Cam uneasy.

"We're *special* friends," Oniyaki said. "I want *Lookout* to succeed. I need good sport for it to succeed. You're good sport. You deliver audience. That matters to me. *You* matter to me."

"Right," Cam said. "Are we all done, here?"

"Not quite," Oniyaki said. "Abby, be discreet when you drop him off, yes?"

"I will," Abby said, looking Cam up and down.

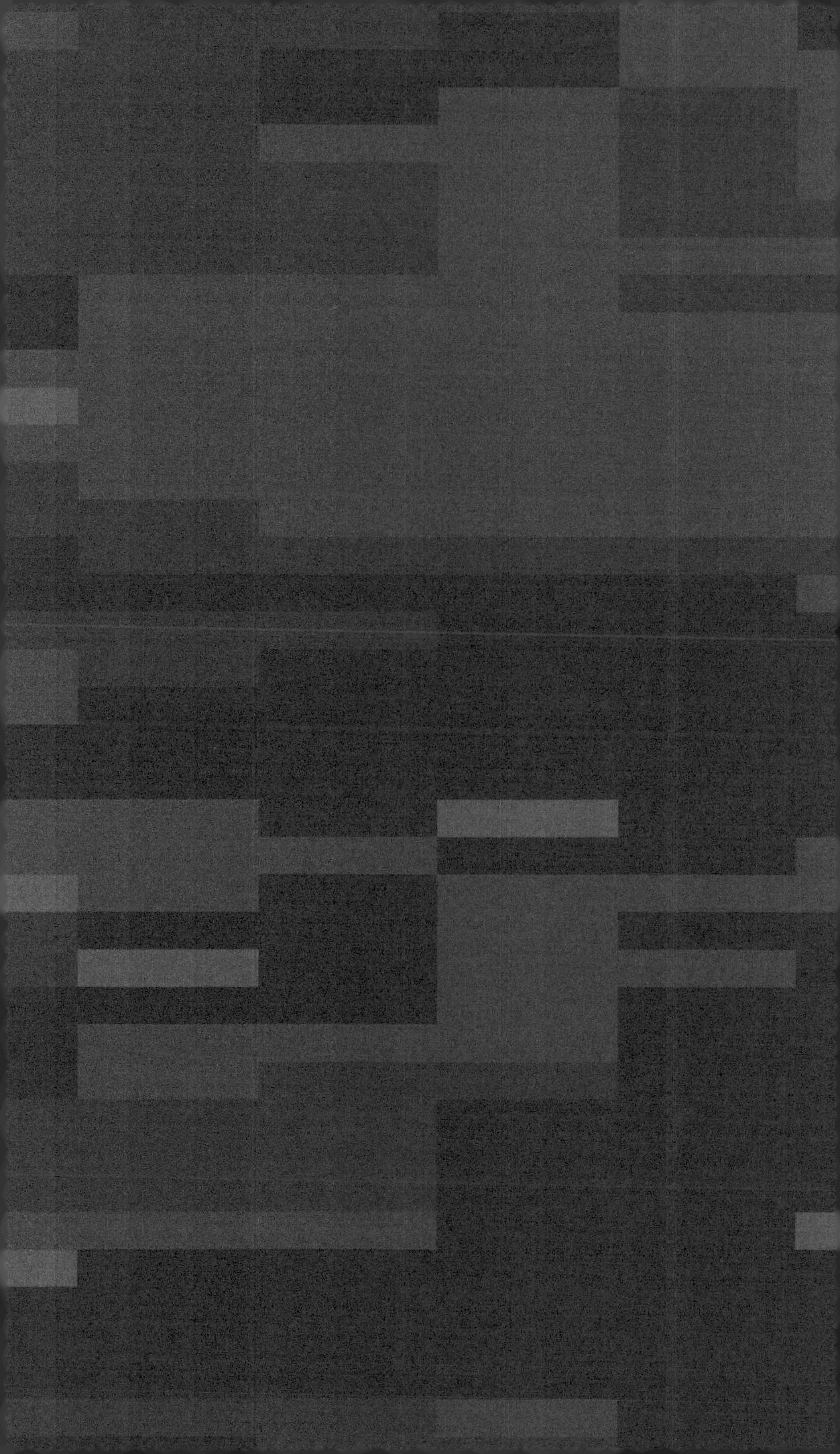

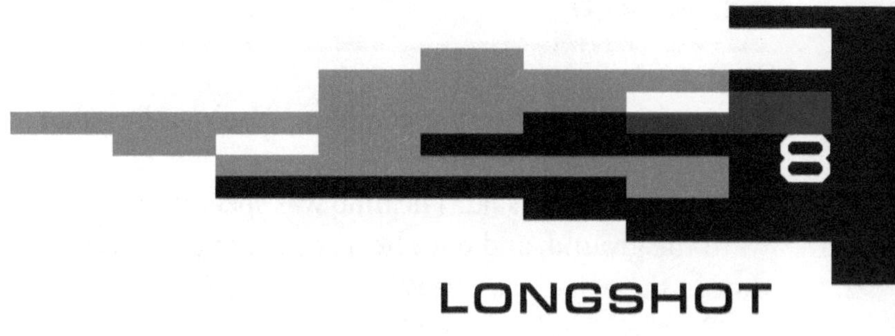

LONGSHOT

Abby didn't say a thing to Cam while they first sped out of Upperton, but Cam took advantage of her quiet to vent to her as they made their way down.

"This is ridiculous," Cam said. "What have I done to piss him off? It doesn't make any sense."

"Live or die, you'll be making him more money," Abby said.

"I can't figure it out," Cam said. "I'm worth more to him alive, don't you think?"

Abby didn't appear convinced.

"Oniyaki is worth a lot," Abby said. "You can't really know what he values. I don't think you're as important to him as you think you are."

"Clearly," Cam said. "Can you pull the Stopper, already?"

"Not until we're at the dropoff," Abby said.

Being cut off as long as he was made him feel a little unglued. Cam couldn't understand how a meatsack like Abby could even operate the way she did, untouched by the Grid, the Matrix, and everything in between.

"You look bad," Abby said. "Shaky. You know once it's revealed that you're the target, the betting will start going up. That's where Oniyaki's really going to clean up.

Viewership, yeah, but the gambling. You're a longshot. I sure wouldn't bet on you."

"Thanks," Cam said. The limo was speedily zipping toward the ground, and once he was out of it, he was on my own in the worst possible way.

"Bit of advice," Abby said.

"Oh, you have advice for me?"

"If you want it," Abby said, almost ruefully.

"Okay," Cam said.

"Don't stop moving," she said. "Get some primo speed and just keep going. Maybe get out of Shytown. Go somewhere remote. Make the clown work for it. You hang tight somewhere and Stabbo will carve his way to you. Three days isn't that long."

"That's a lot of advice," Cam said. "Didn't think you cared."

"I don't," Abby said. "But the longer you live, the more money Oniyaki makes. The more he makes, the happier he is. If it's over too quickly, it'll be disappointing. He will be disappointed."

"And I'll be dead," Cam said. Cam was bitter about all of it.

"The dead don't worry about pain or gain," Abby said.

"I want my gun back," Cam said.

"Once we're out of the car," Abby said. "Here's how that's going to go—I'll drop you off Streetside, and you'll turn your back to me. Then I'll pull the Stopper and give you your pistol back. Then you keep your back to us and count to ten. Do not look back at me."

"Or what?" Cam asked.

"Just don't," Abby said. "In fact..."

She pulled a red silk ribbon from a pocket, unfurling it.

"Put this on," Abby said.

"Wait—"

"Do it," Abby said, and Cam did, even more irritated. She slipped in close to Cam as she tied it, placing a ginger-tinted kiss on his lips that he didn't expect.

"What was that for?"

"For luck. Or maybe it's just the Kiss of Death, Looker. *Lookout* begins the moment that Stopper's out. You go live and then try to stay alive. You'll see the timeclock."

"Where's Stabbo right now?" Cam asked.

"Oh, he's in Shytown," Abby said. "Not so far away for you to get too comfortable."

The limo had reached the street and Abby chuckled, opening the door. Her warm hand reached for Cam's and led him out.

"This is it, Cam," Abby said. She slid the G91 into the back of his waistband and positioned him so his back was to her. "Stopper's coming out in three, two, one..."

And she yanked the Stopper, Cam's sensorium flooding with a momentary backlog of accumulated data that had piled up in the wake of the assassination of Sandra Scene and Victor Glimpse. Fans were concerned about Cam's whereabouts, and there were floods of information, dis-information, and misinformation about Lookers getting bumped off around the world.

Cam saw the *Lookout* clock activate the moment the Stopper was pulled:

[71:59:59]

Cam tore off the silk blindfold and went live, glancing back to find no trace of the Yak flying limo, in a hopeful act of defiance.

"Hey, all, I'm back," Cam said.

He pocketed the silk blindfold and hastened his way across the street as rain fell from another caustic storm rolling through.

"Bit of something going on," Cam said, but fans were already aware of *Lookout,* were talking about it. What Cam didn't expect was a phone call from Stabbo. He picked up, unsure what else to do.

"Hey, Sexton," Stabbo said. "Why don't you make this easy on yourself and just rendezvous with me somewhere? It'll be quick."

Stabbo's voice was rough and scratchy, his face ghastly white, his hair abominable orange as it had always been in his snuff feed. His expression made him appear to be smiling blackly at him, his lifeless blue cybereyes somehow greasepaint-gleeful.

"No chance," Cam said.

"You're damn right," Stabbo said. "Can't figure why some Spiffo like yourself would participate in my kind of fun, here, but choosers won't be beggars, right? What'd you do? Who'd you piss off?"

Cam figured he had a larger fanbase than Stabbo, just because there was always a higher proportion of uprights versus darkwebbers. He sent a ghostmode message to Moxie, who'd been worried about him when he'd vanished. In ghostmode, he could communicate covertly, without being seen by his onlookers. Every Looker had their ghostmode private channels.

Mox, get Devilish on the case. I need a gun printed up fast. Combat auto shotgun. Easy action, variable fire, with recoil compensation. 12-gauge. High capacity. Keyed to me. Interlink Eyeconic 360 targeting compatible.

You okay, Cam?

I'll tell you later. Just get that gun printed, yeah?

I'm on it, Cam. I'm hearing real-time hot goss, Cam. Stabbo?

Yeah, part of what I'll tell you later, I promise.

Cam switched out his Eyeconics to low-light, just for some reassurance as he made his way down the rain-soaked street.

DEVILISH DETAILS
[71:29:15]

The Morningstar Print Shop was practically a Streetside shrine, and was fortunately open at all hours, and Devilish was only too happy to find Cam at his armored door. He stood there behind thick ballistic glass in his red-faced glory, his twin horns protruding from his high forehead, his black goatee beard immaculate. He wore a black suit and a red necktie with a pitchfork lapel pin. His cosmetic surgeon was a wunderkind from Geneva with a wild mind and the steadiest of hands.

Some said Devilish looked handsome, others said he looked like a fool. The Beaters hated him for it, and he'd had to hire a trio of bodyguards to feel safe from them on the rare moments he slipped out of his workshop-fortress. They were three hardwired souls people just called the Fates, who looked identical: all tall and terrible, videographic vixens with long faces and quick fingers and a penchant for silvery shimmer-coats and sleek smartguns always at the ready.

"Cam, you're lucky I was in tonight," Devilish said, grinning at him from behind his security counter, which amounted to him perched protectively on his lavish red-velvet throne rumored to be made from real wood, the

Fates close at hand, with a scrip-n-chip paywall as well as a delivery door right there. "You never come by anymore."

"Apologies, Devilish," Cam said.

"You know, I have to wonder why you'd not just buy yourself a piece," Devilish said. "Why printed? Why a shotgun, even?"

"I wanted something custom I could trust," Cam said. "Do you have it?"

"Slot me and see," Devilish said, and the paywall blinked orange-red. Cam pulled a credcard and slipped it into the slot, not wanting to pay through his headware. Peepers were already announcing it.

Cam's gottagun.
Shotgun Cam.
Shotgunna work on Stabbo?
No way, Spliffs. He is armored.
And fast.
Wicked fast.
Quicker than a wink.
Faster than speeding bullets, Plonker.

The delivery door opened and out came the freshly-printed auto shotgun. Cam took it and held it, pleased by the heft of the thing.

"No shells, though," Devilish said. "But for you, I am prepared. We have slugs, shot, flechette rounds. Preference?"

"All," Cam said.

Cam paid for three boxes of shells, which popped through the delivery door. Cam took them and began loading the shotgun, alternating types of rounds, while Devilish soothingly narrated.

"That's a 12-gauge right there, as requested," Devilish said, over his shoulder. "It has a twenty-round drum and a variable fire mode—single shot, three-round burst, fully auto. As requested, bioprint-enabled based on what we have on file, so nobody else can use it on you. Should play nicely with your target-tracking fancy eyes, if you're actually trying to land some lead on Stabbo. Not that this is going to happen, since Stabbo's just going to go at you with his hands and walk out of the way of your bullets."

"So, you know?" Cam asked.

"*Everybody* knows, Cam," Devilish replied, his opalescent grin widening into a kingly leer. "I'm flattered you came to me first, my friend."

"The devil you know and all of that," Cam said.

"Police see you with that ghost gun and they're going to be holding out their hands for a payoff," Devilish said.

"Cost of doing biz," Cam said.

"You know, that's goofy, you loading up alternating shells like that, Cam," Devilish said. "Somebody like Stabbo, I'd just opt for slugs, I think. Try to punch holes in him, hope you're tracking. You'll like the recoil compensation on that one. Smooth. I threw in the hook and sling for free, you know."

"Thanks, Devilish," Cam said.

Stabbo called him again, and Cam answered, trying to make a note where he was.

"A shotgun?" Stabbo asked. "Come on, Cammo. You think you'll even get a chance to use that thing on me?"

"Better safe than sorry, as I see it," Cam said.

"Like Devilish said, I'll just step out of the way while you're shooting, Slick," Stabbo said. "I mean, I'll just walk around those shells before I gut you. I'm actually insulted."

"Sorry," Cam said, slinging the shotgun over his shoulder. He pocketed the remaining shells, calculating that he had enough for one reload of the drum.

"You're not a soldier, Cam," Stabbo said. "You don't know what you're doing."

Cam was analyzing the shots of Stabbo as he was ha-ranguing him. He looked to be north of the river, judging from what Cam glimpsed. He hung up on Stabbo, while some Peepers chimed in:

Stabbo gonna kill Cam.

No way, Stiff.

Bet?

You bet!

"He's talking to you now, isn't he, Cam?" Devilish asked.

"He was," Cam said. "Gotta go, Devilish."

Devilish waved to him before re-locking the delivery door, the maglocks clanking.

"Good luck, Cam," Devilish said. "Thoughts and prayers, you know what I mean?"

CROSSTOWN
TRAFFICKER
[71:05:05]

Oniyaki had been right about the attention this little deathmatch would bring. Cam's feed was cranking. His fans were flocking, as were scores of Onlookers, Peepers, and Creepers just hopping on to see what was what. Even some Voyeurs were turning up. He could see his sidebar feed capturing the digital snow of their avatars and icons waterfalling. There were Stabbo fans, too, judging from the trash talk on the feed.

Stabbogonna kill you, Pretty Boy.

He's gonna take your head.

You dead, Streetwalker.

Clown's going to town on you, Looker Hooker.

Cam's mind was working as he made his way around town, keeping the shotgun ready as he made his way. The one advantage he had was that Stabbo had to close on him, which he hoped would give him enough time to shoot him dead.

He deliberately mixed-and-matched the ammunition on the shotgun so that Stabbo wouldn't entirely know what to expect. A wirehound like he was would have to plan for three ballistic contingencies instead of simply one. Those moments might be sufficient.

Cam called up a driver using his headware. People were only too happy to be there for him, for their chance at being seen. Everyone loved a Looker if they had an audience, and, thanks to Oniyaki's detonations, Cam had access to plenty of audience who wouldn't have batted their eyes at him before. The difference between third place and first was easily several million audience members, by Cam's estimation.

The live interactivity was part of the draw, too, with various Peeper segments and clusters reacting to the feed—old guard Cam fanboys and fangirls, newbies, Cam haters, Stabbo fans, Stabbo truthers, Stabbo haters, trideo tourists, pervs, Creepers, lurkers, rival Lookers, jaded Stiffs, tripping Squiffs, feral Squids, twisted Spiffs, bleating Beaters, fanatics, fan addicts, stalkers, cops, killers, copycats, and wannabes. It was a ton of eyes on him, and on Stabbo's feed, as well, always watching, hoping for something to see. The promise of blood spilled guaranteed audience.

He was glad he'd gotten the Eyeconics, because people were raving about the clarity of the feed, which was sharper than Stabbo's more utilitarian feed, Cam couldn't help but notice. He didn't know what the clown had for eyes, but they looked to be older models, primarily target-focused, whereas Cam's eyes had a far greater range of views, something he would take advantage of as he worked his way through *Lookout.*

Cam wondered if Oniyaki would honestly let him survive if he somehow won. It was risky to trust a Yak with anything, especially one who'd put an explosive thrall collar around your neck. But Cam thought some semblance of honor existed in the man, and was banking on that, despite what he had done to him.

The driver pulled up, a young Latina woman with a shock of brown-and-blond hair, close-shorn on the sides but a big spray up top and a triplejack behind her right ear. She wore a dark grey jumpsuit festooned with holographic vendorpatches that provided hints of underlit illumination. Vendorpatches were often the fashion among the younger, where favored products were only a touch away. Cam avoided them, as he didn't like the megacorps having greater insights into his buying behaviors than they already did. A Looker he might have been, but he also strangely valued bits of privacy on his own terms.

"Cam Sexton," she said. "I'm Lady Linnea Leadfoot, at your service."

"Hey," Cam said, noting her smiling. She wore red fingerless gloves, and her car was an electric Ford Paragon 68, black-painted with a white racing stripe.

"Hop in the back, Slugger," she said. Cam did, slotting at the payport. "Where we headed?"

"Anywhere," Cam said. "Just keep rolling, and I'll figure it out along the way."

"I can do that," she said, and they took off. The Paragon was one of the high-end electric muscle cars that were often used in the Deathraces run between cities. Only degenerates and dilettantes still used petrol, with grain alcohol being a more favored fuel in the rural Hinterlands. In the city, electric was the go-to fuel option, with some of the more destitute drivers rigging pedal-powered generators to recharge during off-hours.

Her car was street-clean, which meant she had a garage. She was slotted in her ride, only feigned steering, since she was driving with her mind. Any drivers worth their scrip were remote drivers, preferring the road rush they got from cyber-bonding with their ride. There was a hierarchy of ostentation among the driver class, depending on their vehicles of choice and the manner in which they drove. The talent largely broke down along these driver lanes:

ALL-PURPOSE DRIVERS (APDs): As comfortable with any vehicles they drove, whether by land, sea, or air. Very often post-military specialists. Could be counted on to keep cool in dicey situations, and their versatility was a key selling point.

HOTRODDERS: Largely land-based, could drive cars or trucks. Often in the racing business, with a penchant for speed and steadiness, in it for the thrill of the chase. Given their fast-and-furious lifestyle, Hotrodders were very often looking for work, and could be hired on the fly with a desire to get a passenger where they needed to go in return for some ready scrip.

FLY GRRLS & FLY GUYS: Air and space, always post-military. They were the real speed freaks among the drivers, tended toward high-end gigs, not so much Streetside. Most of them were employed by Upperton Swankers and couldn't be bothered with land-based work, and worked through talent brokers and fixers, never getting their hands dirty with off-the-shelf work.

TANKERS: Ground- and sea-based heavy rig operators. Either post-industrial and/or post-military, they traded in a hardcore "get you there" kind of mentality, relying on durability over speed. Tankers were employed Streetside around the world and took a certain pride in their stubborn drive to get where they set about going. Tankers were good road-fighters, as many of them were hired in rural Hinterland routes that required stoic ferocity.

RE-CYCLERS: Specialists among the Streetsiders, these motorcyclists were their own brand of speedsters, liked to pretend that they were flying through the city streets. With the highest body count among the drivers, Re-Cyclers earned their name because of their knack for ending up scooped off the streets by Ghouls and processed for parts. Still, if one was suitably desperate, a Re-Cycler at the right time could be just the speeding ticket.

DRONE JOCKEYS: While the other drivers might look down on them because they were remote from their vehicles of choice, Drone Jockeys were always thirsting for gigs and many of them were as good (or better) as direct drivers, which was a sort of dirty secret among the driver set. A primed Jockey could pilot multiple vehicles simultaneously, with the best of them running gigs with three or more vehicles under their control. Those commanded the highest fees, and often Jockeys piggybacked with other drivers on gigs, with plenty of them moonlighting with combat drones and/or gun turrets. Most often post-military.

Regardless of what they drove, drivers had a taste for amphetamines of various strengths and could tolerate levels of the drugs that would lay out most tossers. While all drivers carried optics as well as communication and sensory arrays, plenty of them at the higher end were tricked out with haptic interfaces that let them really cook with their vehicles of choice.

"Ah, okay," Cam said. "You're rigged up, yeah?"

"I am," Leadfoot said, as she sped them through downtown. The Paragon rolled quietly and smoothly. He figured her for a Hotrodder or an APD, judging from her rig and how she carried herself behind the wheel.

"This is a nice ride," Cam said.

"Nothing but the best for you, Cam," she replied.

"Is it armored?"

"Of course," she said. "Ballistic glass, hardened frame, runflat tires. She's good for city and suburbs and cross country, you feel me?"

"Battery life?"

"Five hundred kilometers," Leadfoot said. "I have a solar rig in the trunk for recharge, as well as rollers on the wheels I can engage to keep her charged up while I drive. We could run her for days without stopping if we had to."

"Tempting," Cam said. But he knew Stabbo wouldn't go for that. He didn't want to put the young driver at risk. She glanced at him through the rearview mirror.

"I'm game if you are, Looker," Leadfoot said.

"What's your car's name?" Cam asked, smirking at her. She glanced back at him, their eyes meeting a moment. Every driver he'd ever known had named their vehicle.

"Sheena," Leadfoot replied, and some of Cam's audience weighed in:

Sheena is a cyberpunk rocker.
WTF are you even talking about, Stiff?
Forget it.
Done.
Sheena's the dirty girl next door.
Like your mom?
Hey, I should know, Spliff.

Cam took a moment to catch his breath in the back seat. He wasn't sure how Stabbo would play it, exactly. He had just under three days to find and kill Cam. Maybe he would take his time with it, milk it for the audience and the gambling that would occur.

To that end, Cam peered at the betting pools at Casiknow™ that were springing up around *Lookout*. He was the longshot bet, for sure, with a 50-to-1 odds of surviving the episode, while there were currently 1-to-1 odds that Stabbo would find and kill Cam. There were 100-to-1 odds that Cam would kill Stabbo, instead.

"Thanks for the vote of confidence, everybody," Cam said. However, he just needed to survive. If he could successfully evade Stabbo, he could make a killing. He threw

100K chits on himself, betting his own survival from one of his cash stashes. As he saw it, why not? If he died, it wasn't like it was going to matter, anyway. He just needed to avoid being killed. He threw 25K chits on him killing Stabbo. Fans were watching and commenting on it.

Cam's here to play!
Cam's here to stay!
Cam's out to slay!
He ain't clowning, for sure.
I don't get it.

His headphone rang again and he picked up, even though it was Stabbo yet again. Cam ran it audio-only, figuring the cyberclown was already staring through his eyes.

"You killing *me*? Hahah, that's rich, Looker," Stabbo said. "I swear I'm going to gut you for that."

Cam looked at his own feed, could see that he was heading south.

"Your souped-up sweetheart isn't going to be able to keep you safe, Cam," Stabbo said. "I've got people bearing down on you right now. Part of Stabbo's Streetside Cyber Circus."

Cam whipped his head around, peered out the back window, could only see other vehicles making their way. Nobody stood out.

"Don't worry, you'll know, Pal," Stabbo said. "You've got balls, I'll give you that."

Cam gonna kill the clown!
Get bent, Spliff!
Clown's gonna slice-n-dice Cam!
Stabbo gonna put Cam's eyes in a Marstini and drink'em down, Plonker.

There was no point in negotiating with Stabbo.

Leadfoot kept them rolling, the Paragon running smoothly. Cam wondered what Lady Leadfoot did to afford a ride like this. He did a quick dossier crawl, one of those speedy searches he often did while out Looking. Leadfoot made her scrip as a driver-for-hire, anywhere, anyone, anytime. That clinched the APD classification as far as Cam was concerned.

She'd invested in the improvements of her Paragon ride to increase her marketability. The Paragon came from her father, who'd been a mechanic, had taught her everything he knew before he'd been killed during a Beater riot when she'd been on a job for Terradynamic. Since then, she'd pushed her driver gigging hard, earning a reputation as a solid go-to for rig gigs.

"Uh oh," she said. "I think we've picked up a tail."

Stabbo laughed, a baleful sort of cackle.

"Scratch that, I know we have," Leadfoot said, pouring it on. Cam looked back again and there were two trucks rolling hard for them, what looked to be pickups painted pink.

"Pinkies inbound, Looker," Stabbo said. "Enjoy the ride."

Stabbo hung up on him, while Leadfoot kept rolling.

"They're gaining," Cam said.

"I see them," Leadfoot said. "Remember, we're talking city traffic, here, Cam. I can't go all out here."

She yanked the car to an exit at the last minute, which tricked one of the pursuing trucks, while the other whipped after them harder. Getting closer, now, Cam could see the trucks were packed with Stabbo wannabes—fanboys wearing white facepaint and trailing pink and orange balloons. They were brandishing spiked clubs and chains. The bed of the pickup was packed with them, hooting and hollering.

"You strapped in?" Leadfoot asked.

"Yeah," Cam said.

"Good," Leadfoot said. She did a powerslide through a changing light and barreled hard right on the rainy road.

"They're not going to risk shooting us," Cam said. "Because that'd cut into what Stabbo's angling for. But they will harass."

The Pinky pickup came on strong, tailgating them. Cam wondered if the driver was rigged the way Leadfoot was, or if he was doing it manually. The pickup certainly had some chops, judging by how quickly it was driving.

"Yeah, alright," Leadfoot said. "Check it, Cam."

She had a sunroof, which slid open smoothly. Next to her, on the passenger side, Cam saw a little drone rise up. It was a quadcopter model, sleek and black, and whirred to life, rising up through the open roof.

"You're driving and flying that thing?" Cam asked, doing a mental reassessment of Leadfoot's abilities. Maybe a Drone Jockey was in there, too. Either way, it was impressive.

"Multi-tasking, Looker," Leadfoot said. "You know how it is."

Cam unbuckled and popped his head up through the sunroof for a better view. He saw Leadfoot's drone flit over to the Pinky pickup, clamp onto the front of it with mechanical arms, and pop the hood. Going the speed it was, the hood flipped right up, blocking the view of the driver, who slammed on the brakes, to the delight of Cam's audiences.

Damn straight! Drone on!

Cheap tricks, Stiff.

Pop that top, Leadfoot.

Then Leadfoot had the drone clip some cables in the exposed engine, which looked to be an old ethanol motor. Stabbo's hardcore fanbase was pure corn-fed ethanol, from the look of them.

The drone detached and flew after Leadfoot and Cam, while some of the Pinkies got out to try to fix their pickup, cursing and cackling in equal measure. Cam assumed they were all drugged up psychophants, anyway. A thrill was a thrill, regardless of how it came one's way.

"Nice one," Cam said.

"Herbie's good for repairs on the fly," Leadfoot said. "But sabotage is just repairs in reverse, as I see it."

"Is that a philosophy?" Cam asked.

"It is, now," Leadfoot said, grinning at him through the rearview mirror.

The drone flew back as a big truck slid in beside them. Cam could see the white-faced creep behind the wheel, another of Stabbo's fans.

"Where are *my* fans, dammit?" Cam asked. "Stabbo's got an army."

"Maybe your fans aren't drivers," Leadfoot said. "Or, you know, they're less psychotic."

Herbie flew in and landed beside Leadfoot, while Cam fished out his shotgun. The trucker blew his horn, which blared loudly in Cam's face.

He used his targeting system to lock onto the truck's front tires, which caused the trucker to give them some space.

"Yeah, that's right," Cam said. "Back off."

"Brace for a left turn, Cam," Leadfoot said, and Cam did, and she did, the Paragon's tires squealing over the wet road. Overhead were the antiquated Helltrain tracks, the lost pride of Shytown from the ancient days.

The big rig truck slid in after them, honking. Again, Cam speculated whether it was an analog driver or someone rigged up. The low-fi nature of Stabbo's fan base made him think the man was analog, which ought to have given

Leadfoot an edge in a pinch, but that was perhaps offset by the truck itself.

"Get back in here and buckle in, Cam," Leadfoot said. "I'm buttoning up."

Cam flipped off the trailing truck and hopped back to his seat, while Leadfoot closed up the top with a flick of a switch. Cam watched the cover cut off the cloud-clotted sky with a funereal finality.

"Alright," Leadfoot said. "Gonna ditch that rig on our six, Cam."

She spun the wheel, the Paragon knifing rightward, and sped them east. She went a block, then cranked her wheel left, and they were going north. He thought maybe she was putting on a little show with her steering, since she was still jacked into her wheels, moving it with her mind. If it hadn't been life-or-death, he might have fancied jacking into her rig and seeing what she was seeing and feeling. He parked that on a shelf for a future livecast, thinking that might tweak his fans.

"It doesn't matter," Cam said. "There'll be others. They're tracking my feed."

"How about you look at your feet, maybe?" Leadfoot said. "Stop being so damn observant."

Cam was amused at the suggestion. His instincts were to give a good show, but with Oniyaki hijacking him for his *Lookout,* there was that possibility that he might just try to mess with the onlookers by closing his eyes awhile. That would be particularly amusing as he kept the feed live, as people could hear what he was hearing, but not see anything. He filed that away for future use right next to the driver feed.

"I don't know if I can do that," Cam said.

A message was beamed to him, a coded and anonymous one that made him think it was probably Oniyaki:

You're right. You can't.

"Well, alright, then," Leadfoot said. "I could take us outside of the city. Those country roads, we could really haul ass, Cam."

Some of his Peepers chimed in.

Spike strips ahead, Cam. Townie Clownies from Bushwhackistan.

"Best turn off," Cam said. "Strips ahead."

"I've got runflats, like I toldja," Leadfoot said. "But I gotcha."

She turned right.

"Where's the Shytown Metropolitan PD?" Cam asked. "I would've thought somebody would be on us by now."

"They're probably too busy betting, Cam," Leadfoot said. She wasn't wrong. The cops were fitful in their enforcement of the law, depending on a variety of factors—who was straight, who was crooked (and for the crooked ones, who was their patron—you'd get a very different reception depending on whether you were dealing with a Yak, Triad, or *Bratva* cop), what part of town you were in, what day it was, how much scrip you were worth, what the cop's mood was. All sorts of things. Self-service was the rule of the day where law enforcement was concerned.

"Does this car fly?" Cam asked. Leadfoot laughed.

"Not yet," she replied. "I don't have that kind of scrip for that."

"Too bad," Cam said.

"Where are we headed?" Leadfoot asked.

"You can drop me off at the Plunderdome," Cam said.

"Southside safari, got it," Leadfoot said, spinning the wheel again as she drove the car even faster than before.

WELCOME TO
THE PLUNDERDOME
[69:41:32]

The Plunderdome was the acknowledged open-air black market of Shytown, a former sports arena in the ancient days turned into a kind of shitshow shantytown by the locals, who flocked to the place to do biz and trade scrip, chits, and everything else they could get hands and eyes on. Anything worth having could be had at the Plunderdome, except for a clear conscience.

It was a hulking presence in Southside, a temple to trade, and the clusters of shacks that had grown around it like the way coral once did in oceans made it look almost organic. It had solar-powered spotlights that would cut lines across the sky, rain or shine, and draw people to it. One part carnival, one part thieves' market, entirely questionable, it was about the worst place for a person to go, which was why Cam went there without hesitation.

There were semi-permanent trade tents that went down the length of it, crafted from old olive drab macrocanvas that was designed to handle any weather—rain, wind, sleet, snow, sun—and offer protection. Nobody quite knew where it came from, but speculation went to some enterprising smugglers working with the Polygon to acquire milspec surplus. Beneath the billowing sheets suspended by tubing of aluminum or bamboo were the vendors, whose voices haggled and barked constantly, offering deals, a chorus of buying and selling.

Domers were a tribal sort, and they took care of their own, which meant that while the Yaks and Triads took a bite from every trade that was made—the covenant was that everything to the north went to the Yaks, everything south went to the Triads, in terms of tribute—anybody there could be counted on being left alone, free of fear of predation or interference from any of the local gangs operating outside the friendly confines. While it was not quite a sanctuary, for any bizzers out there, it was at least a comprehensible place where anything worth having could be had, if one knew which stall to frequent, which merchant to tap.

For Cam, the Dome was a good place to get his head together and buy some time. With all the activity, the literal hustling and bustling taking place, it would provide him what amounted to cover.

The Plunderdome was run by Danny Leviathan, a local fence who had made all the right friends and enemies in the course of his decades-long career. He worked with anyone and everyone who came to him, which was a profitable business model.

Leviathan was a big man, a fat man, with pale skin, bulbous eyes and a wide mouth filled with diamond-dusted teeth. His laugh was like a klaxon, and he was well-protected by two noteworthy street samurai—Thumbelina, a revved-up, chalk-white, sharp-toothed doxy with twin monofilament thumbs she used to slice into cutlets anybody who crossed her, and Lancette, a Black Amazon assassin with a penchant for perforating her targets with a diamond-tipped hewing spear that had been custom-printed at great expense by Devilish.

People thought she was crazy for using it, except that she was wired so tight she blurred when she fought. There was a certain unspoken cred gained among the street sams in choosing a melee weapon over the more mundane firearms and flechette weapons. Because any Spliff could (and would) use a firearm, the use of more primitive weapons by a street sam was a status symbol, with the implication that they were so revved that they could use such antiquated weapons and still win in a fight.

Plus, since only outright nutters would bring swords, knives, staves, spears, or bows and arrows to a gunfight, those who did had to be particularly dangerous because they were so clearly out of their minds, or too confident and cocky to care. They dealt in death and weren't afraid of it, looked it right in the face, up close and personal, street sam-smirking all the while.

Cam didn't traffic much with street sams, who were invariably mad, bad, and dangerous to know. They were always chromed to the hilt, which meant that wherever they went, there was trouble. And given that violence was their brand promise, they were not given to much in the way of senses of humor. This meant that Cam gave them a wide berth, since all he would need was for some chatty audience member to make some offhand comment about a street sam for it to escalate. Street sams were more like forces of nature in Shytown—rumored to exist, but ideally never quite directly seen.

That said, Cam had stolen glances at a few in his day. There was Fast Jack, who had been on-tap at the Plastic Fantastic a time or two as hired muscle. He'd been strangely dapper for a street sam, with a pronounced favor for purple, blue, or green suits of ballistic cloth, and a grey fedora he always wore. His face was masklike, with lethal-looking eyes that were probably doing ballistic calculations of patrons of the club. Fast Jack was ostentatious in his minimalism, which made him a particularly dangerous street sam.

Streetside logic was that the more chromed-up a sam was, the more they were trying to compensate for something. The swaggering tanks one sometimes saw were the real kooks, whereas a lean sam like Fast Jack communicated two things to observers: 1) he had first-rate gear that didn't require a hefty body-build; and/or 2) he didn't need all of that chrome to get the job done.

Some believed that Fast Jack was a bluffer, since the man only carried a vintage military dagger and an Argosy 10mm flechette pistol, and plenty of people thought Fast Jack was full of it. That was sorely tested one night at the Fantastic, when three chromed street ruffians who went by Three of a Kind: Whipsaw, the leader, this coastal chrome junkie with flingblade forearms and a loud mouth; Conniption Fitz, Whipsaw's second, a southern screwtop chrome dome with ludicrously large cybernetic arms that promised punishment and pain to anyone he got his hands on; and Immodesty Blaze, Whipsaw's squeeze, who had a pair of handguns that were wired to her cybereyes and gave her a daunting kill count in her day. The three of them all dressed alike and even looked alike, wearing black vinyl coveralls and combat boots, their heads shaved bald and bearing black eye makeup.

They'd barreled their way into the Fantastic, clearly jonesing for a brawl with Fast Jack.

"Fast Jack," Whipsaw said, his augmented vocals audible even over the music. "Challenge, Plonker."

Cam had been there with Moxie, the two of them in an armored booth overlooking the always-packed dance floor, the two of them watching the scene unfold. Cam was gleefully recording it, naturally.

"What's going on, Cam?" Moxie asked.

"Something wild," Cam replied, altering his eyes to deal with high-speed activity, which was the right thing to do at the right time, as Fast Jack and the Three of a Kind went at it. In retrospect, the actual exchange only lasted seconds, but to Cam's eyes, it was a bloody battle undertaken in scores of steps, as the reflex-revved combatants went at it.

Whipsaw unlatched his arms, the scything blades flicking out at Fast Jack, who sidestepped them and threw his knife at Immodesty Blaze, the blade sinking deep between her startled cybereyes before she got a shot off. Conniption Fitz swung at Jack, who ducked below the powerful haymaker, having drawn his Argosy, firing three tight shots at Fitz's collarbone, above the close-fitting body armor he wore, but below the subcutaneous lattice he wore to shore up the massive cyberarms the man had. Because it was a flechette pistol, it was quiet, making only the faintest coughing of sounds as the coiled magnetic repulse weapon unleashed the needles into Fitz. Cam knew that flechette weapons had a myriad of darts they could use. Judging from how Fitz buckled from the shots, he wagered that they were poisoned darts.

Fast Jack's face was impassive as he yanked the dagger from Blaze's head, even as Whipsaw was trying to bring his arm blades down on Jack. The bouncer darted away from the descending arm blades, firing two perfectly aimed flechette darts into Whipsaw's eyes, each needle finding its mark in the center of the proverbial bullseye, blinding the Streetside tough before he even realized it. In another motion, Fast Jack brought up his dagger and buried it in Whipsaw's throat before the mouthy merc could even let out a yell.

"Whoa," Cam said, snapping back to ordinary optics, which had Fast Jack standing over the Three of a Kind, all dead at his feet. For the barest of moments, Jack flicked a glance at Cam, before saying something to the bartender. It had all happened so quickly, so quietly, that the patrons had hardly noticed, as the hapless trio were carried out of there.

"What just happened, Cam?" Moxie asked.

"Just Fast Jack, taking out the trash," Cam said, watching the Three of a Kind vanish into the shadows. He'd caught all of it, and got a ton of play out of that lopsided fight he'd captured. He and Moxie slotted where they sat, sharing in the replay.

Cam needed a sam with the finesse of Fast Jack, but sams were a tricky lot where hiring was concerned. Some could create as many problems as they solved.

If he was lucky maybe some would come to him—everybody knew Cam was arriving, and a holographic jumbotron used for Plunderdome pit fights had been given over to their feeds, a splitscreen between what Stabbo was seeing, and what Cam was looking at.

When Cam and Leadfoot rolled in, cheers went up among the Domers, a sea of losers and wannabes yearning for even a glance from the Looker. Most of the Domers were desperate for scrip, attention, and infamy, and would do whatever they could to get any.

"You're so famous, Cam," Leadfoot said. "Maybe some entrepreneurs will try to steal Stabbo's bounty."

"Maybe," Cam said, hoping nobody did. "Thanks for the ride."

Cam paid her extra for her trouble, and she appreciated it, judging from the cock of her eyebrow as she tracked the chits.

"You ever need a lift, you ring me, yeah?" Leadfoot asked, glancing at him over her shoulder. "Anytime, any-place, anywhere."

"You know I will," Cam said, hopping out.

The Domers milled around them at distance, vaga-bonds and thirsty souls eyeing Cam and his shotgun with greed and wariness. He thought maybe some bold ones might make a play as Lady Leadfoot drove away, as small-er spotlights dance across the approach, alternately bath-ing Cam in light and drowning him in darkness. Domer drones hovered on quadcopter wings, watching with their dead camera eyes.

But then the crowd parted and Thumbelina strolled up, looking him over. She was impudently youthful, with bright red eyes and bright blue hair that hovered over her brow like a breaking wave. She wore a baby blue ballistic jumpsuit and a bone-white fur stole that Cam assumed had to be fake. Thumbelina wore only one vendorpatch, that of the White Whale, marking her as Leviathan's, the hologram glowing white and underlighting her pretty face.

"Danny-man wants to see you straightaways, Looker," Thumbelina said, playfully tugging one of her monothumbs. The filament caught the spotlight glare like a sliver of a rainbow. "The Whale wants to know why you come downwise here, yeah?"

"Lead on," Cam said. Thumbelina strutted beside Cam, hooking her arm through one of his while spotlights fixed on them and drones danced afterward like an entourage. Even a walking soon-to-be-deader like Cam was a celeb-rity while he was still kicking.

"Shooting star turn runway walk-n-talk with a walk-ing dead man," Thumbelina said in a whisper in Cam's ear, giving his arm a squeeze. Up close, her red eyes were brighter than life, and Cam thought maybe they were

Eyeronic 880s, boring into him, scanning every detail as surely as he was scanning her. Love at second sight.

With Thumbelina escorting him, Cam felt reasonably certain he'd make it to Leviathan's pad, but three of Stabbo's clown army had a go at them, anyway—they were juiced-up bruisers, dead end dragoons with nothing to lose—one tall and lean, one short and mean, one big and bad. Cam's Eyeconics could all but see through them—the wild eyes, the amphetamine-twitches, three young men with greasepainted faces and clown-comic colors of blue, green, and orange.

"Yo-yo, Looker-Hooker," one of them said, the Mean Green. "You goin' the wrong way. Stabbo's thatward."

He pointed back the way Cam had come. He was the big one, the alpha of this trio. Shorty, the one in orange, nodded, grinning, pulled out a metal basher bar painted bright yellow.

"He's got the right of it," Shorty said. "Back the way you came, Cammer-Jammer."

Thumbelina, however, wasn't having any of that, while drones danced around them, catching glimpses.

"We're off to see the Whale, Spliffs," Thumbelina said. "You *really* want to get all up in our waylay, hey?"

The lean one in blue drew a stunstick, one of those crackling police batons packed full of voltage. The blue arc of the electricity crackled as he thumbed the switch.

"Sure looks like it, Thumbs," Blue said.

"Alright," Thumbelina said, giving Cam an Eyeronic wink. "Blink and you'll miss it, Cam."

Cam raised his shotgun but Thumbelina shook her head. Cam knew she was relishing being so close to him, wanted to milk it for the Peepers. She let loose her thumbs, which dangled on their monowires, catching the light, while Domers formed a hooting circle around them.

The three tried to flank Thumbelina, who twirled her wrists, making her thumbs spin and form a pair of whirring circles with the monowires.

These days, nobody with half a brain remaining risked playing with razorwire that way, but Thumbelina wasn't the type to care, and, to Cam's eye, she knew what she was doing, as she quick-whipped Mean Green, who'd rushed them, her right thumb cutting the man in half before he got two steps toward them, while Sparky, as Cam dubbed the guy with the stunstick, tried to block her left thumb fling, only to lose both his hands as the rainbow ribbon cut through his wrists. He let out a howl, even as Shorty took off running.

Not content to let him go without a memento, Thumbelina flung both her thumbs at Shorty like she was casting a spell and lopped both his ears off as the twin wires creased his skull to either side, to the cheering delight of the crowd, who were scrambling to scavenge the remains of Mean Green, the stunstick, Sparky's twitching hands, and Shorty's ears. The Plunderdome's meat market would accept them all. The remains did not remain long.

Thumbelina drew her thumbs back in while the crowd applauded, and she did a few little bows before hooking her arm back through Cam's as if nothing had happened.

"Did you catch all of that splat-a-tatter, Cam?" Thumbelina asked, a breathless whisper in his ear. She liked getting close.

"Oh, I caught it," Cam said.

"So glad," Thumbelina said, giving his arm a squeeze. He could see her fingernails were painted an eclectic electric blue that played nicely with her hair.

Of course, what Cam had witnessed was getting played and replayed by Peepers, with a vigorous commentary about the efficacy of monothumbs, and whether Thumbelina was a poser or the real deal street samurai.

Bad enough to have one, but a deuce? Cray.

She cray, she slay for pay.

I'd do her.

She'd do you, turn you to wagyu.

Stabbo called Cam yet again.

"Cute," Stabbo said. "But that gutterskank samurai won't get in my way, Cam. She's all thumbs."

"Wasn't planning on that," Cam said.

"The Whale won't save you, either," Stabbo said. "Nor all that Domer trash. What are you up to?"

"You'll see," Cam said.

"Yeah, I will," Stabbo said. "I'll see you soon."

He hung up on Cam, while Thumbelina walked them toward Flukie's, Danny Leviathan's club and bunker, a multilayer concrete cake illuminated by a flat-roofed white neon whale that had a tail that flipped up and down in a progression of lights. It was at the equator that divided Yakland from Triadville, almost qualified as an embassy of sorts.

"Nobody even knows what whales are, anymore," Cam said.

"They're big fish that breathe the breathy airwise, yeah?" Thumbelina said. "For breakers and shakers, only. Flukie's been around too long by half, Cam. The Whale doesn't make the rules. He's an institution."

Flukie's was situated in the center of the Plunderdome, mounted on five stout pillars that kept the riffraff from strolling on in and gave Leviathan a lordly sort of authority in the heart of the Dome. There were two sets of stairs that led up, both populated by a dozen bodyguards, all of them wearing white suits and armor. Even their guns were white. Cam flipped a gazed to see if they were wired, and it appeared that some were, but nothing anywhere near what Stabbo had in terms of gear. He'd have cut through them all like they were nothing.

They were eager to catch Cam's eye, posing as Thumbelina brazenly worked him past them, her hips swinging with each strut up the steps.

"Ordinary-like, they'd frisk you rightish downwise to the bone, but The Whale understands you're not here for troubleshooting, Looker," Thumbelina said, walking him up, her hand on his back.

Cam could see all the eyes on him as he glanced back, the sea of Domers hoping for a glance. His feed hummed, his onlookers in greater number than ever. Drones weren't allowed to fly over Flukie's, not too near, anyway, so they hung back, watching and buzzing.

Dead man walking, alright.
The Whale won't save him.
The Whale gonna eat him.
Thumbelina HOT.
CAM hot.

Cam smirked as they reached the top, despite himself. Lancette was waiting for them there, her bright blue eyes boring into him, her spear catching light on its diamond tip.

"Danny's inside," Lancette said. "Leave the guns with me, see?"

"I see," Cam said, handing the shotgun and the G91 to her outstretched hands. He could see a diamond knife at her hip, Lancette wearing a white silk kimono with a black cat embroidered on her back. She was tuned up much like Thumbelina was, revved to be able to sidestep bullets if she wanted to. Lancette saw him noticing and gave him a wink.

"The Whale's a'waiting, Looker," Lancette said.

IN THE BELLY
OF THE WHALE
[69:19:36]

Flukie's was the fanciest club in the Plunderdome, for Streetside VIPs only (nobody higher in the statusphere would have dared to turn up there), which put it at something of a midrange establishment in Cam's experience, with blue seats and white tables around its ballistic-windowed perimeter with a circular bar in the center, underlit by white neon. Another matching neon white whale adorned the wall over the bar, flipping its tail over and over again. Whether it was smashing something or merely trying to swim wasn't something Cam thought too much about, and that absence of reflection caught up with him in that moment.

Thumbelina guided Cam in, while Lancette strode alongside him, both of them jockeying to ensure they caught some of his gaze. Being a Looker meant being seen, and Cam imagined those mock-Triad bomb boys blowing up Sandra and Victor, how easy it had been for Oniyaki to send them on their way. It gave him pause, but thankfully, there were none like that he could detect. Then again, assassins weren't meant to be spotted until they appeared, which made them the bane of Lookers everywhere.

In the heart of the bar was a circular tube, indicating an elevator, which was attended by another bodyguard, a hulking young man in a white suit and white tie, who looked Cam over without a smile, his cyber traceries creeping above his collar and dancing on his cheeks. Cam figured reflex enhancements, maybe some combat mods. Skillports likely among his datajacks, letting him punch above his class.

He stepped aside, the three of them entering the elevator, which only had five buttons on it. Thumbelina pushed the top one, waited for the identification algorithms to clear her, and up they went.

In the close confines of the elevator, Cam looked them both over, the two of them trying to appear coolly uninvolved while fully aware of his attention. Lancette's fabled diamond spear had somehow shrunk. It was slung across her back, now. Cam was displeased he'd missed the weapon's transformation. He hated missing things.

"You two want some bodyguard work?" Cam asked.

"We're not available, Looker," Lancette said.

"Not that way, anyway," Thumbelina said, giving him a poke in the ribs he felt through his armored jacket.

"Yeah," Cam said. "Just thought I'd ask."

The elevator door opened, and they were in the Plunderdome penthouse of Danny Leviathan, a sea of white furniture on a floor of glossy black stone. The black and white of the place was, to Cam's eyes, a blend of Leviathan's embracing the underworld so forcefully that he could afford to have immaculate white furnishings devoid of Streetside grit—he was an artisan of both grime and crime.

"Cam Sexton. Take a seat, Looker," the Whale said, grinning at Cam from his divan, a half-dozen white-suited bruiser boys nearby at the bar. Leviathan was wearing a voluminous white silk robe, barefoot, eating a platter of vat-grown oysters on a low-slung table in front of him. Wallscreens were tracking his own and Stabbo's feeds.

Thumbelina sat next to Cam, while Lancette hovered nearby, handing off his guns to one of Leviathan's men.

"Thanks, Danny," Cam said.

Leviathan wore his ample weight as a kind of badge of success—in a world packed with starving people, the man could afford to be fat. It spoke to his opulence, and even extravagance. His skin was bone-white, and Cam was confident that it was bullet-resistant. Hell, even the fat may have been a few layers of kinetic-absorbent tissue that would prevent even some armor-piercing high-velocity rounds finding their way in. The decision was a cheeky one, since so many hustlers in Shytown and beyond sought to look sleek and slender, whereas Danny Leviathan embraced his corpulence as part of his branding. He kept his head bald, which, to Cam, felt like another act of aesthetic rebellion on his part—the man could have afforded a beautiful mane, but opted to be bald. His cyber-eyes were a glossy black, without pupils and irises evident, which, when paired with his perfect-toothed leer, made him particularly menacing, like he was in on a joke only he could tell.

"You want a drink? You look thirsty," Leviathan said. "Get this man anything he wants, Chumbo."

Chumbo the bartender was a service hoverbot, like two spheres of chrome, one bigger than the other, the smaller one serving as a head, where his face rendered in a digital display of blue dots approximating a face. Chumbo smiled and acknowledged with a voice processor. While bots were everywhere, most operated behind the scenes, instead of out in the open. What played on a factory floor or in a headphone was less-welcome at service settings. Too many people associated bots with violence, and while nobody in Shytown could afford to be squeamish, a bot more often than not was seen as a weapon. Cam was confident that Chumbo had weapons in that spherical chest of his.

"Right away, Sir," Chumbo said. "What'll you have, Friend?"

"Détente," Cam said. "Extra ice."

"Détente it is," Chumbo said, quickly mixing the drink. Leviathan watched Cam watching with amusement. The two of them had history, in that each knew who the other was, which counted more than it didn't in Shytown.

"I trust Chumbo, drinkwise," Leviathan said. "He's beyond reproach, programmed not to poison me. Always important."

"Brave words from a man eating oysters. But you're doing alright, looks like," Cam said, glancing around. Leviathan chuckled, slurping an oyster. Cam assumed they were shipped in from somewhere very secure, since he couldn't imagine anyone taking them from the oceans these days.

"I've done worse," he said. "What are you doing here, Cam? You going to, you know, finish down here? I mean, you've only just begun, by the look of things."

"Was thinking I'd shack up a night, to be honest," Cam said.

Leviathan looked pleased by this, while Chumbo hovered over and delivered the Détente to Cam, who accepted it and took a drink. It was perfect. Thumbelina ordered a Spit & Kiss, while Lancette abstained.

"I'm honored you'd considered the Drome for your hoteling needs, Cam," Leviathan said. "Although I can't imagine why you'd get out of Downertown for something like this."

Cam wasn't about to share his strategy with Stabbo and all the other Peepers looking in. It was for him to know. Suspense had to count for something, even in Shytown. All Lookers understood this intuitively. The ones that didn't lost audience, and, ultimately, their lives and livelihoods.

"I don't know, Danny," Cam said. "A fella can just be himself in the Plunderdome. Nobody cares who and what you are."

Leviathan laughed, the klaxon sounding, while downing another oyster.

"You know I'm betting against you, yeah?" Leviathan asked.

"Yeah, I know," Cam said. "Most everybody is."

"Just so we're straight," Leviathan said, his black cybereyes glistening. "You really want to shack here? At Flukie's?"

"You've still got rooms, yeah? VIP suites?"

"Always," Leviathan said. Cam was certain the Whale was already thinking of how his presence here would boost biz. That's what Cam was counting on—the Whale was greedy, and right now, Cam qualified as a commodity being briskly traded. He sought to work that to his benefit.

"Perfect," Cam said. "Put me down for a night."

"Only one?" Leviathan asked.

"All I need," Cam said. He glanced and saw that Stabbo had opted to drop in somewhere downtown. His own Peepers were chiming in about it.

Stabbo's gone to Crucible.

Fancy.

Lacey Styrene works there.

And?

Just saying.

Midtown trash.

Crucible was a Midtown drug bar, a place where the jacked got jabbed—that was its selling point, since the hybrid endocrine systems of the otherwise augmented posed challenges in the realm of pharmacology. Cam had been there a few years ago, hadn't been overly impressed by the retro-postmodern neo-brutalist design of the place, the derm bar, the jab rooms, the huff-n-puffers paying scrip-n-chits for clean drugs and cleaner air, and the sea of wannabes hoping for some bizzos to come their way.

That Stabbo went there was kind of strange to Cam—did it pass for high class for him, or was it maybe a nod to the human being he'd once been? Cam made a mental note to think about it more when he had the chance.

The Whale looked Cam over, wiping his meaty hands on a white cotton napkin. Near as he could tell, despite his big boy body, the Whale was only minimally chromed, undoubtedly made enough money to get himself a brand-new body if he wanted one. That he didn't always struck Cam as paradoxical. Cam switched to his SeeThru™ view, which let him assess bioware and cyberware, which flicked right onto the wallscreens, showing the Whale in silhouette, his cyberware visible—headware, eyeware, ballistic blubber and skin, nothing more. The SeeThru™ offered a tidy little dialogue box, identifying the ware: headphone and digital uplink and quad-mounted datajack.

"Now that's just rude, Cam," Leviathan said, without appearing to be offended. "Switch back, you nosy Looker."

Cam went back to normal view, but not before glancing at Thumbelina and Lancette, who were lit up like biotechnological bonfires, quickly catalogued by his own system:

Thumbelina: Two monothumbs, milspec-grade enhanced musculature, advanced reflex enhancement, headware, triple datajack feed, basic pain blockware, adrenaline booster, Eyeronic 880 eye arrays with target-tracking and low-light, combat enhancement assessment, milspec-grade ballistic skin, combat-capable fangs.

Lancette: Elite enhanced musculature, milspec-grade reinforced skeleton, advanced reflex enhancement, headware, double datajack feed, pro-grade pain blockware, adrenaline booster, skillwire combat choreography module with hand-to-hand and melee specialization, Ey-eronic 760s with thermographic and threat assessment mod, basic ballistic skin.

"Sorry, Danny," Cam said. "I just had to take a peek."

"Looker's gonna look, I know. Nobody will stop Stab-bo, you know that, yeah?" Leviathan asked. "Not Thum-belina, not Lancette. Nobody around here will lift a finger for you."

Cam felt insulted that the Whale even had to say that.

"I know that," Cam said. "But at least here, I can keep the tossers from bothering me. Stabbo's got a lot of Spliffs on-call 24/7, you know? Here, I can rest easy, knowing you won't let them get too close."

"Sure, sure. TresPeepers will be shot," Leviathan said, laughing again. His laughter was like a baritone bellows, forced out with heavy pushes from his diaphragm. "But when HE shows, that's, you know, showtime. I don't want you messing up the place."

Cam smiled at the Whale, eyeing the white all around them yet again, taking stock. So much white. It had to have cost him plenty of scrip over the years to get it all. Cam couldn't even imagine the sourcing of it, let alone the maintenance. It was ironic to see it in the cesspool that was the Plunderdome.

"No worries, Danny," Cam said, knowing that they'd all love to see it go down up close, with proverbial front row seats to his own execution.

"Thumbs, you can get him keyed up in the Loft, hows-about?" Leviathan said. "Great view up there, Cam."

"Thanks, Danny," Cam said.

Thumbelina smiled as Chumbo served her drink.

"Happy to do it, Boss," Thumbelina said, giving Cam a sidelong look and a wicked grin.

THUMBSCREWS
[68:07:48]

The Loft was nice for the Dome, as Cam had expected it would be. He was sure it was wired, too, so the Whale would know everything that went on in there. He could see the drones flitting outside, keeping out of range of Flukie's autoguns, but still jockeying for a glimpse of the hapless doomed target that he was. Everyone wanted to take a bite out of him.

Inside was a polyform flip-bed, a datastation, a chair, a wallscreen, a whitewood dresser, a bath-n-shower tube. It smelled good to Cam—like boutique citrus he'd sometimes whiffed in Midtown—and he worked the flip-bed with a switch, while Thumbelina clacked her way through the unit.

"You're *lucky*, Cam," she said. "The Whale likes you."

"I'm likeable," Cam said.

"I like you, too," she said, eyeing him up and down while he slipped off his shoes—hard-soled tactical walkers he'd picked up months ago. They had steel toes and the heels each held a pair of punch daggers that were shielded from most scans. Shoes that were popular among smugglers, and while Cam wasn't a smuggler by trade, he certainly knew how to smuggle himself when he needed to.

It had started raining again, with lightning this time, knifing the sky while thunder rumbled in protest and/or approval. Thumbelina watched, silhouetted by the night's sky, a sinuous shape among the fervent, flashing shadows.

"Bizzos gonna get soaked straightaway," Thumbelina said. "But then they always do, the twankers."

Cam tossed his armored black leather jacket to the chair and dropped back on the polyform bed, taking a moment to rest. He'd tossed his mirrored shades on the nightstand, while he keyed the wallscreen.

"That *real* leather, Cam?" Thumbelina asked, eyeing the jacket.

"As a matter of fact, it is," Cam said. She stroked the jacket with a pale hand, feeling the fabric, lips parted as she no doubt was assessing how much it cost him, where he had gotten it. Secrets that were his, for now. Leather—real leather—was a luxury. The Hinterland tanneries were heavily-armed enclaves, just like any corp-farms and greenhouses were.

"The Whale wants me here all night, Cam," she said.

"Yeah, I figured," Cam said. "Keeping an eye on me."

She glanced at him, lit again by lightning. In the dark of the room, her red eyes glowed, and he thought maybe she was scanning him. He returned the favor, and she laughed—a sharp, carping sort of sound that was part languid lust and part jaded, half-hidden desperation. Cam's profession had attuned him to reading people's expressions and postures, their breathing and blinking as windows into what mystics might have referred to as their souls.

"You're funny," she said. "For a Looker, I mean."

"You've known many?" Cam asked.

"Not nearly enough," she said. "What you do, I mean. Stupid."

"Is it?" Cam asked.

"Yeah," she said, slipping out of her jumpsuit, peeling it off like it was skin. Cam took her in with his Eyeconics, the high resolution sending his fans into fits. She was beautiful, like a statue, artfully sculpted lines that were street-clean and combat-crisp. He could see the tracery of the circuits that fed her frame. Cam wondered what would have taken her down that path, although he already knew the answer—somehow, it had allowed her to make a living, and she'd taken it. He understood that impulse, the drive toward making oneself marketable in Shytown. Nobody Streetside had the luxury of simply being themselves.

While she was lovely, the more risky street samurai path offered her actual power in the Plunderdome, and in Shytown, power meant profit and respect. She was good enough at what she did to earn a reputation, and that reputation earned her still more cred. It was a virtuous circle in Shytown as much as it was a death spiral; the key was knowing when to jump off.

"You're pricey," Cam said. "Who paid for all of that work?"

"The Whale," Thumbelina said. "He's generous."

"I'll bet," Cam said. She gripped one of her thumbs and gave it a tug, drawing forth the line that caught every lightning flash and held it in its golden monowire embrace. "I have ask you—the thumbs, I mean, what happened, there?"

Thumbelina laughed, walking up to him, kicking off her heeled booties while toying with her line all the time. Monofilament lines were a Shytown fad that came and went over the years, both a status symbol and a winking nod to artful obsolescence. Few were insane enough or desperate enough to risk acquiring, let alone using them. There were plenty of tales of unimaginably dreadful ends for victims of monolines, evenly spaced between their users and victims.

"I gave them up," she said. "I mean, who needs thumbs?"

"Everybody, actually," Cam said. "Like opposable, you know?"

"Meh," Thumbelina said. "I mean, like, meat. This way, they earn for me. Everyone's gotta have something up their sleeve these days, Cam. You gave up your eyes, I gave up my thumbs."

She drew back in the spooled line, wiggled her thumbs for emphasis, and pivoted smoothly on their polyacrylic sockets, with an enviable range of motion.

Cam couldn't exactly argue the point, but looking at Thumbelina as she loomed over him, he knew from his scan earlier that she'd given far more than her thumbs. She fast-handed his pants off, working like a blur with her revved reflexes. Cam had known plenty of wired folk over the years, and the preternatural way they moved was like a fever-dream, made stronger still by the strobelight flash of lightning.

"You gave up more than your thumbs," Cam said, and she laughed again, like it was good sport. For those who'd swapped meat for chrome, it was always that rueful acknowledgement that whatever they had been before, they were no longer, anymore.

"Only what I didn't need," Thumbelina said, crawling onto him, taking her time, which Cam knew from his Eyeconics wasn't something that came naturally to her. She kissed him, hard, and he felt her sharp teeth and her tongue stud toying with his tongue as she went.

"Where'd you come from, anyway?" Cam asked, between kisses.

"I'm Pente-Coastal," Thumbelina said, straddling him. "Floodwater basin basic bitch, leastways. Shytown made all kinds of sense, worth the trip and the risk, yeah? Water to burn, leastways. And so *fresh*."

She rode him while the storm raged outside, Cam's eyes upon her in staccato light flashes between lightning crashes, annoyed at the Peepershow he was giving all the onlookers, thanks to Oniyaki and his stupid rules. He figured the damned Yak was watching even now. Maybe the secret bosses of the Triads were even tuning in, as well. Not that he hadn't done as much or worse before, for paying patrons, but this romp felt voyeuristic even by his Looker-low standards.

Cam reached up and held her breasts in his hands, while she gripped his wrists in her too-strong hands, fueled by that custom-cutware that amplified her speed and strength. She could break his hands off with a twist of her wrists if she wanted to. She could have been a choice digital doxy but had gone the martial route instead of diving headlong to the mattress, which was, perversely, something Cam found that he could respect. It took a mélange of guts and madness to take the street samurai path.

"Stabbo's gonna carve you up, Cam," Thumbelina said, between moans and yelps. Her manner was penthouse pixie-playful, and if they weren't in the Plunderdome, it might have been more sybaritic than the carnal coupling that it was.

"So I keep hearing," Cam said. "Maybe I'll surprise everyone."

"There's no surprises anymore," Thumbelina said, as she came hard, right on cue, letting out an animal wail that lingered amid the thunderclaps, very nearly rivaling them. Cam followed suit with his own, but without the noise, only gazing up at her lightning-laced frame, perfectly cast, like she'd been steadily poured from a thermonuclear mold.

"Quickie," Cam said.

"For we revvers, *everything's* quick," Thumbelina said. "We're on another timescale, Cam. You cut what you see into a hundred pieces, and we're many thousands of slivers."

"You're a poet, Thumbs," Cam said, earning a swat from her that made him almost see stars, if he'd had organic eyes. As it was, it was only a momentary static cut in the feed, to the elation of his audience.

Cam's in a jam.
Putting the MMM in Thumbelina, y'all.
Sister's a twister.
Pale but not frail.
Rewind, replay, repeat.
Rewind, remind, rescind, reskinned.
The Plastique Fantastique.
Never been there, myself. Good?
Ecstatic shock and awe.
Sure, Spliff.

Cam pulled Thumbelina to him and kissed her firmly, which made her smile, her biting his tongue with her off-the-shelf fangs she'd no doubt picked up at a custom bodyshop because she thought it was badass, which it kind of was. Plenty of Streetside tossers had cosmetic fangs, but Thumbelina's were of another order, being battle-hardened and designed to inflict pain or poison, depending on her mood.

"The meat wants what it wants," Thumbelina said, without irony, between feral kisses.

Cam checked his headware messages, saw that Nimble had pinged him, as had Moxie. Oniyaki be damned, he toggled his ghostmode on message review, which would allow him to see his messages without anybody else being able to peer at them.

Nimble: You're an idiot to participate in this deathmatch. No leads on Wren, BTW.

Moxie: Be careful at the Drome, Cam. They're setting you up.

He wanted to tell Nimble what Oniyaki had told him but told himself he'd handle it after dealing with Stabbo.

"OMG, are you checking your headmail in this magic moment?" Thumbelina asked, prying loose of him, red eyes flashing.

"I'm multi-tasking," Cam said. "Mind over matter and all of that."

"Ha," Thumbelina said, drumming her fingertips on his chest. He had a tattoo of a black heart over his heart, which she traced. "That's a stupid tattoo."

"Is it?" Cam asked. "It's for the MedEvac people, to help them find their way to my heart."

Thumbelina laughed, maintaining the speedy, ethereal drumbeat with her fingers.

"MedEvac would never get here in time," Thumbelina said. "If you needed help."

"I have a platinum contract with them," Cam said. "They're at least supposed to try. I'm counting on that."

Thumbelina nodded, playing with one of her thumbs, which made a quiet whirring sound as it unspooled, the length of monowire glimmering in the intimate dark while the driving rain fell outside, like it was otherworldly. Which it was, in its own monomolecular way. Materials science techs were always coming up with new alloys, materials, molecular structures, at least behind the confines of the megacorporations. Cam had a conspiracy theory he privately toyed with that the megacorps would sometimes let bits of tech out on the street, just to see what people might do with it outside of laboratory conditions. They were fanatical about their intellectual property rights, but it didn't mean they were averse to field testing when the moments were right.

There were, in fact, a whole subclass of corporate Lookers like Glimpse who were on the megacorp payroll who might track and monitor new product releases, offering field evaluations and tracking user interaction and unintended consequences of the new tech. Corp Lookers tended to stand out, as they were always well-kept and didn't have public audiences the way the Streetside Lookers operated. They worked for clients covertly, on dedicated, proprietary feeds. Sometimes those bled out (literally and figuratively) across other channels, but mostly they operated behind firewalls, within closed circuits.

From Cam's perspective, that was soft work. Steady, sure, but lacked the juice that he savored with his own freelance bizzing. A corporate Looker was a caged bird—Cam and other Streetsiders called them Lookies and Looksies as a slam. They went where they were told to go, looked at what they were told to look at, saw what they were told to see. The trade-off of that short leash was that they tended to get good ware, which was why when the Eyeconics had become available, Cam had lunged for them. They were Lookie-level ware, which made them a prize worth snatching up. Cam was fortunate in his friendship with Doc that he even gave him first dibs on those. A more mercenary street surgeon might've staged an auction for them, which would have gotten expensive, bloody, or both.

Thumbelina stroked him with one of her cool hands, bringing him back to the moment. Street sams always had cool hands, owing to their tech. Chrome was cool to the touch more often than not. Most of them went with it as a kind of status symbol—cool hands and colder hearts.

"You live large, Cam," she said. "I respect that."

"Yeah?"

She let the length of monowire lay against his chest, softer than a spiderweb. He couldn't even feel it as she slid it along his skin, shearing off some hair as it went. It was a strange sensation, at once terrifying and arousing, tapping into some animal part of his brain that understood he was in danger, but that selfsame danger arousing him. Limbic foreplay.

"You going to exfoliate me?" Cam asked.

She lifted it and let it drape over his neck, near the explosive collar. The monowire felt cool for a moment before soaking up his own body heat. The right flex and his head would come clean off. He tried not to sweat it, but sweat beaded on his forehead just the same.

"Hey, now," Cam said.

"Nobody would see it coming," Thumbelina said, leering at him, showing her teeth. "Like nobody."

"No money in that," Cam said. "And since you didn't know I was coming to the Dome, you wouldn't have wagered on it."

She straddled him again, looking down the end of her nose at him, holding him down with her other hand, fingers steepled against his chest while the monowire hung across his neck. Cam had never had anybody toy with him with a monowire like that and wasn't about to reveal how unnerved he was by it or how turned on. Cam understood the peril bad habits presented, which was why he conducted himself with a degree of decorum that was noteworthy even Streetside.

"Maybe I surprised you," Thumbelina said. "Maybe I was enterprising, Cam. Scheming, even."

"You really want to dance with Stabbo?" Cam asked, while she rode him again.

"I could take him," she said. "Leastways, I'm not scared of the clown."

"I don't know," Cam said. He didn't know how much force or pressure a monowire required to do its job. Not much, from what he'd seen over the years. He switched to thermographic vision to see Thumbelina's body heat. Something for the fans to gawk over, something to distract himself from his own distraction.

She cray.

Monowire'll take Cam's head clean off.

Thumbelina gonna kill Cam, take his head as a souvenir.

MedEvac can fix that.

The hell you say.

Cam's ice cold, Thumb's white hot.

Cam felt the weighted thumb slip to one side, and before it could slice into his neck, Thumbelina pivoted her wrist and reclaimed it, smirking to herself as she rolled her hips again, while Cam's hand went to his neck.

"There'd better not be a scar," Cam said.

"Don't be such a baby, Baby," Thumbelina said, red eyes looking orange in the thermograph, giving off some heat, but not as much as the rest of her as she came again, throwing herself back and then forward, lips near his ear. "If I really wanted to mark you, I'd do way better than that, Cam. I'm the sort of girl who knows how to make her mark, you know?"

"Is that what I am? A mark?" Cam asked. He savored wordplay, enjoyed those who played along. It was the mark of an active mind, and Cam liked that, wherever he encountered it. With all the draggers and the slaggers out there, it was a nice change of pace.

"You're a Cam, Cam," Thumbelina said. "You could never be a Mark. You're making your mark, as I see it. That's more something than nothing, leastways. Sit still, now, and let me mark you, Cam."

She nipped his ear with her fangs, then gave him a lingering kiss to make it all better.

MIDNIGHT IN WHITE SATIN
[63:21:08]

Cam only realized he'd been asleep when his headware rang. It was Stabbo. Cam's timeclock told him it was just past midnight. He glanced at Thumbelina, who was asleep, curled up beside him. Street sams always slept lightly, but she seemed genuinely out at that moment.

"What is it?" Cam asked.

"You sleeping, Cam?" Stabbo asked.

"I was," Cam said. "What do you want?"

Stabbo looked to be looking out over Shytown from someplace high up. The city looked like a field of pretty lights of blue, orange, pink, red, and green—traceries and points of light.

"Did you think I was coming for you last night?" Stabbo asked.

"Kinda did, yeah," Cam said.

"Too easy," Stabbo said. "Part of the fun is watching what the prey does, like where it goes. You shacking with the Whale, I don't know. Can't say I saw that for you. You seem too Midtown for that kind of play, Cam."

Cam didn't know whether to be flattered or insulted, and Stabbo chuckled.

"I'm full-on Streetside, you know? Born and raised," Stabbo said. "I never had anything better. Soldier was the only thing that made sense. Made me what I am today."

Cam wondered what Stabbo was up to, here. Was it some ploy? Or was he toying with the nightowl audience, the Creepers and Peepers who might be lounging on the feed, doubtless buoyed by abundant pharmaceuticals.

"You're a killer," Cam said.

"Exactly," Stabbo said. "Good at it, too. When the show came up, I jumped at it. Stupid not to. A guy like me, the chance for that kind of reach? No-brainer. But you? Seems a stretch. A bad fit."

The late-night crowd were getting wind of this exchange, were commenting to each other about it.

Cyberclownin' around, Spliffs.

Stabbo taking stock, is all.

Cam's dead meat. Stabbo wants a taste.

Just a whiff.

"I had no choice," Cam said. "I'm the one with the explosive collar, you know?"

"That you are," Stabbo said. "Anyway, we had at least three million watching yesterday. Those are good numbers."

"Yeah, they are," Cam said.

"My forecaster thinks we might break five million before it's done," Stabbo said.

Cam was impressed by that. To date, he'd never gone much past a million audience at his best. In a world of fractionated attention spans and segmented psychologies of fans, that kind of reach was solid.

"Pretty sweet," Cam said.

"They're just watching in hopes that I'll get to it," Stabbo said. "It's like a wave, you know? Peaks and troughs. I've got sixty-three hours left in which to kill you. The question is where the audience will go, like more or less. If there's an audience dropoff, maybe we'll have a problem. We'll have to escalate."

Cam could see where he was going. Street he may have been, but Stabbo understood something of showmanship. Looker life required a sense of it, at every level.

"What I've done before, the snuff stuff," Stabbo said. "It's not much in the way of foreplay, you know? You go right for it. This is more of a dance for me, I don't know the steps, how to make it last."

Cam smiled to himself, while outside, the rain raged.

"The longer it goes—up to a point—the more wagers you get," Cam said. "The more people speculate. The more peeps you get. The greedy gaze. The lustful looks."

"Yeah," Stabbo said. "So, I'm thinking we need to meet up, you and me. Face-to-face."

"Ha," Cam said. "You think I'm an idiot?"

"No, I don't, actually," Stabbo said. "I think you're smart. Which is why I think you'll do it. We conduct the hunt the way *we* want, you and me, you feel me? I think a sitdown might scratch a helluva lot of itches."

Cam could only imagine what was going through the cyberclown's head, but, for some reason, he thought maybe he'd not just kill Cam outright. Stabbo understood there was a mechanism or process here. The mechanics of showmanship meant more money for him if he played it well, if he drew it out.

"How about lunch?" Stabbo asked. "Someplace fancy. You pick."

"Lunch?" Cam asked. "Not dinner?"

"Dinner if you want, but lunch seems, I don't know, less of a commitment," Stabbo said.

"Stratospherical," Cam said. It was an Upperton place.

"Stratospherical," Stabbo said, laughing. "Nosebleed central. Right in downtown Upperton. You do like rubbing their faces in it, don't you, Cam?"

"Yeah," Cam said, already making the reservation for four.

"Four?" Stabbo asked.

"Yeah," Cam said. "You, me, my agent, Moxie, and your agent."

"Serpentina," Stabbo said, laughing. "They'll have fits at Stratospherical."

Stratospherical had a riffraff firewall in place for reservations, but lunch had a window they could thread, and Cam's willingness to throw chits at them allowed him to bypass the algorithmic paywall that ordinarily would have kept people like them from getting anywhere near it.

The Stratospherical AI engaged them both. It was a pale blue androgynous face that gazed at them with eyes like sunshine.

"Gentlemen," Stratospherical said. "We have a strict dress code, even for lunch, and a no-kill policy for patrons. Acceptance of the reservation requires adhering to our dress code and behavior guidelines."

"Fine, fine," Stabbo said, laughing to himself. Cam agreed as well. "Tina's not going to like it, but I'll talk her through it."

Cam was already beaming an update to Moxie.

"Are we good?" Cam asked.

"Oh, we're good," Stabbo said. "Sweet dreams, sweet prince."

Cam set his head to Do Not Disturb and slept like the dead while thunder rumbled and lightning slapped the sky around, and his audience yammered back and forth about his fate on their lunch date, making wagers, taking numbers and talking trash.

LOSING ONE'S HEAD
ABOVE THE CLOUDS
[52:52:52]

When word beyond the latenighters had gotten out about Cam's lunch date with Stabbo, fans went crazy. The creepers had spouted on it directly, and as the rest of Shytown woke up, things were positively phosphorescent on the gambling front.

Thumbelina had been properly peevish that Cam hadn't invited her to Stratospherical, but the Whale had been understanding, had laughed long and hard about it as Cam had reclaimed his guns and snagged a ride downtown in the midday fog, having arranged a meetup with Moxie at the Uplift.

He'd picked up a suit along the way, opting for black suit, black tie, like he was going to his own old-time funeral. Moxie had worn a tight black silk dress with white piping and looked thrilled to see him still among the living. Cam had stored his shotgun and G91 in one of the StreetLockers™ near the Uplift, pocketing the card key, hoping no Stabbo fanboys jumped him in the meantime.

While officially part of Upperton, Cam knew the real Upperton action was in orbit. The landbound Upperton offerings were primarily for the lowball strivers who sought to feel above it all and were willing to pay for the privilege. Anybody who was anybody understood that high-rise Upperton was just a jumping-off point for far more grandiose things—the sort of things one needed telescopes and advanced optics to see.

"Cam," Moxie said, giving him a hug, her monocle whirring with scrolling updates. "So glad you made it out of that hellhole intact. Hope you slept well."

"Mostly," Cam said, as they went into the Uplift.

"I thought that Thumbelina was going to kill you," Moxie said.

Cam smiled at Moxie, earnestly peering at him through her monocle.

"Occupational hazards, Mox," he said, making her roll her eyes.

"I've never been to Stratospherical," Moxie said, as they were let into the elevator.

"Me, neither," Cam said. Her mind was working, and her blue and purple hair looked freshly-tended. She smelled like cloves and sandalwood to him, smells he knew by name only, or because someone had told them that's what they were.

Her blue eyes flicked over him, and she smiled with worry and excitement. As his agent, she was paid to feel that way.

"Great audience numbers so far, Cam," Moxie said. "Over three million onlookers in the past twenty-five hours."

"Right," Cam said.

"The sitdown was inspired," Moxie said.

"All Stabbo's doing," Cam said. "I think he likes the high life."

"If this even qualifies," Moxie said. "You know, he's a lowlife, Cam."

"Aren't we all?" Cam asked.

The Uplift was gold and white, Art Deco, nano-clean and overseen by a bulbous overhead camera that was glossy black and likely would have pumped the elevator with nerve gas if they did anything undesired.

"My ears are popping," Moxie said.

Cam's were, too, but he kept cool. Upperton always made him uneasy. While the people who lived there—and higher, still, out in orbital arrays in what was known as the Heights—were made of money, life in the Heights always made Cam uneasy. He preferred to have his feet on the ground. The people who lived in the Heights were most often only felt, seldom seen, by design. Their money spoke for them.

There were a number of space elevators around the planet, all heavily guarded. The enterprising Southard-Hamlin company had engineered space elevators to allow for effective space travel, using highly classified supermaterials capable to weathering the stress of deployment. Cam had never gone up one of those, but as he was on the Uplift, it made him think of that.

Moxie, of course, noticed his unease, and commented on it.

"You okay, Cam?" she asked. Her voice was comforting, crystal-clear with client-care tones. Cam wondered how her tone might shift if and when he lost his audience share. He banished those thoughts, not wanting the high-value audience members soaking up that emotional vibe. Even keels made for better deals.

"Fine," Cam said. "Never better."

"You look uneasy," Moxie said. Cam decided to make her commentary work for him, build up some audience tension.

"We're only about to meet with the man who's planning to kill me," Cam said. "What's to worry, right?"

Moxie thought about it, more worry creeping on her features while her monocle HUD scrolled through scenarios. Her monocle was so adorably out-of-place, it was character-defining. Nearly nobody used them anymore, and Moxie's embrace of them gave her a distinctive vibe she worked wherever she went.

"He wouldn't, you know, ambush you here, would he?" Moxie asked.

"You never know," Cam said. "I mean, with cyberclowns, you *never* really know."

The term "cyberclown" had arisen over the years as both a descriptor and a slur that had been almost defiantly owned by those who'd earned it. Unlike the more elegant-sounding "street samurai"—the cyberclowns wore their hefty number of body modifications with an almost burlesque and defiant enthusiasm. They'd been made into mod-monsters and they reveled in it.

The first generation of cyberclowns had appeared among veterans of the World War IV, especially in Fragistan, where their respective militaries had heavily modified their frames, including the common use of polyflage skin modification that tended to turn their skin complexion bone-white when they weren't using adaptive camouflage to evade detection.

It was something more complicated than Cam cared to understand, but the logic was that the incorporation of all possible skin pigments defaulted to chalk white unless a color was selected. The handful of surviving cyberclowns out there simply owned it, becoming distinctive specimens—green-haired Bingo, orange-haired Stabbo, red-haired Fraggo, blue-haired Bizzo, and purple-haired Killjoy were the five most prominent cyberclowns still in operation. There was the added benefit that their existence terrified the Fragistani population, and so the militaries who had spawned them ran with that idea, using them as bogeymen to terrify the locals in a particularly ruthless bit of PsyOps.

What was perhaps more interesting was that the militaries who had created the cyberclowns ultimately left them alone, as attempts to reclaim their costly modifications typically met with violence. None of the surviving cyberclowns could live normal lives without their mods—their bodies had been so completely ransacked by the biotech cybernetic processes that built them that they could no longer go back to any semblance of normalcy. If one's body was a temple, the cyberclowns were desecrated beyond repair and any hope of salvation.

That's what made them so distinct. While any ordinary street sam could never hope to blend in with normies, there was at least the possibility that they might, if they really wanted to, rebuild and replace their bodies. For the cyberclowns, there was no possibility of normalcy ever again, even when they rolled off service.

The Polygon had attempted to reclaim Bizzo when Cam was a teen, and it had not gone well for the tactical teams, as Bizzo had made literal mincemeat out of the mercenaries they'd used to try to rein him in, and an entire city block in the soggy BosWash metrosprawl had gone up in flames before Bizzo went underground. That attack had led to all of them following suit, slipping below the radar, popping up at odd moments, taking gigs when they needed them.

In the wake of the Bizzo disaster, most complicit militaries opted to wait out the cyberclowns, quietly reclaiming their ware when they died of natural causes—or when they died in combat, which also qualified as natural causes among cyberclowns.

Because of the heavy amount of modifications they had, cyberclowns were always down for biz. The upkeep was always an issue for them, and most of them had slid far below the grid, out of sight, almost urban legends. Bingo made his name as a sniper-for-hire, while Bizzo worked protection rackets for the Triads. Fraggo was still employed by the Polygon, while Killjoy, the only remaining female cyberclown, lent her services out as a top-shelf assassin, and Stabbo made his name working the stimsense snuff circuit as a flamboyant vigilante/bounty hunter.

Cam watched them reach the 500th floor and the doors opened with a chime. Out they stepped into an immaculate lobby, the Vista Lounge, an Art Deco apostrophe that was where people could occupy themselves while waiting for Stratospherical.

The floor looked to be white marble, with real green-fronded genuine (!) trees in decorative pots scattered around golden embroidered chairs and sofas, while overhead was a gilded dome cut with little wedges of glass. A crescent-shaped bar hung to one side, tended by a handsome bartender.

Up here, the sunlight actually shined, lancing through the glass and bathing the Vista Lounge in unfamiliar illumination. Cam could see the pretty patrons lingering around with their drinks, everyone stunning, whether through cosmetic surgery or biomechanical engineering.

"Oh, my, Cam," Moxie said, gripping his arm a moment. "Are we on the right floor?"

"We are," Cam said. "It's that way."

Cam thought the patrons were pretending that they didn't notice Cam and Moxie there, but he was fairly confident at least some of them knew who he was and why he was here, and were hoping for a glimpse of the Looker, the Walking Dead Man.

"Let's get a drink," Cam said. Up here, the security wasn't readily apparent, but he knew it was there. They were being monitored through any number of discreet cameras. He toggled his SeeThru™ mode and watched it track a dozen countermeasures in the Vista, trending toward targeting optics and flechette guns. Flechettes were always favored for their quiet, so as not to disturb patrons.

"I do love a day drink," Moxie said.

Cam ordered a Détente for himself, while Moxie had gotten a martini, her eyes bright and dazzled by all the light.

"It's so shiny up here," she said.

"Nothing but the best for the best," Cam said, sipping his Détente, raking his eyes over the patrons, who looked old-young to Cam, and whose abundant mods were identified by his SeeThru™ gaze. Nobody ever looked honestly or voluntarily old in Upperton. He could only imagine how bad it was up in the Heights. Any of these fancy people would have been carved up for parts if they set foot down Streetside. Fortunes could be made from any one of them.

"Is Stabbo here?" Moxie asked.

"Not yet," Cam said, monitoring his feed. Stabbo looked to be making his way to the Uplift. He was glad he'd at least gotten there before Stabbo. Maybe it was all a setup—maybe the cyberclown would come out of the Uplift and would sink his stabby fingers into Cam, making him bleed out on the floor of the Vista Lounge. Wouldn't that have been a sight?

But he didn't think so.

The Vista Lounge patrons just watched, none of them deigning to approach. In truth, as Cam saw it, these people were the riffraff of Upperton. The real players were in orbit or even offworld. Anybody slumming it here was just another class of Spliff, when you really thought about it.

Cam refused to allow himself to be intimidated by them. He was a somebody among the nobodies, and that made him better than these Strivers, who were anonymous nobodies among the wealthy somebodies. Enough scrip-n-chits to gain entry to the entryway, but not much past it.

The Uplift opened, and out came Stabbo, wearing an electric blue suit that played well with his shock of slicked orange hair. He grinned at the sight of Cam and Moxie at the bar, winking at the Strivers who gawked at him. He was a tall man, and he moved with a jaunty smoothness that reflected the perfect calibration of his reflexes. He'd zeroed everybody in the Vista in moments and had a powerful presence that made Cam feel even more like he was a dead man. His SeeThru™ told him why:

Stabbo: Milspec-level ballistic polychromatic skin, high-tensile concealed handclaws, Eyeconic 730 armored optics with reactive FlashGuard™, target tracking calibrated to battlewired reflexes (combat-grade) as well as low-light and thermographic, combat oversight integrator, milspec-level armored skeleton, elite-grade strength enhancement, high-powered pain blockware, top-shelf adrenaline enhancer, spec ops-grade blood filtration, EMP-hardened headware scrambler, quad datajack feed, headware.

"You like my setup, Cam?" Stabbo asked, grinning at him.

"Impressive," Cam said, toggling off his SeeThru™ view.

"Expensive," Stabbo said.

Stabbo was handsome in his strange way, with well-cut features that radiated a magnificent confidence. It was as if he was some sort of superman run through another lens, with a different color palette. He could kill everybody in the Vista without even thinking about it. Cam estimated it would have taken him under a minute to do it, without so much as breaking a sweat.

Beside him was Serpentina, who was herself a vision in body modification, her emerald eyes set with reptilian irises and a golden skin that betrayed ballistic scaling. Her hair was an elaborately coiffed updo that looked like spun gold, and she wore a shimmering green minidress that clung to her every curve. She wore green heels that made her stand as tall as Stabbo, and Cam could see her green fingernails were both long and sharp, circuit traceries going all up her lean arms, while golden snake bangle bracelets danced at her wrists. An agent she may have been, but Cam thought she could have been a killer, too. Maybe that's how it worked for somebody in the orbit of a cyberclown.

Absolutely everyone in the Vista was watching them pass.

"Oh, my," Moxie said.

"Cam," Stabbo said, snapping his bone-white hand out shake. He saw that his fingernails were painted orange, and Stabbo's cybereyes were brightest blue. Cam reflexively shook Stabbo's hand, which was very cool to the touch. "Glad you could make it. This is Serpentina, my agent."

"Charmed," Serpentina said, holding out her hand for Cam to shake. He could see she'd gotten boutique fangs as well, completing her look. Her hand was surprisingly warm to the touch. He wondered if her tongue was forked, as well.

"This is Moxie Monocle," Cam said. "My agent."

Stabbo shook her hand, smiling at her, while Moxie actually blushed.

"It's an honor to meet you both," Moxie said. "Really and truly."

"Fuck all these Stiffs, Cam," Stabbo said. "Let's get to it."

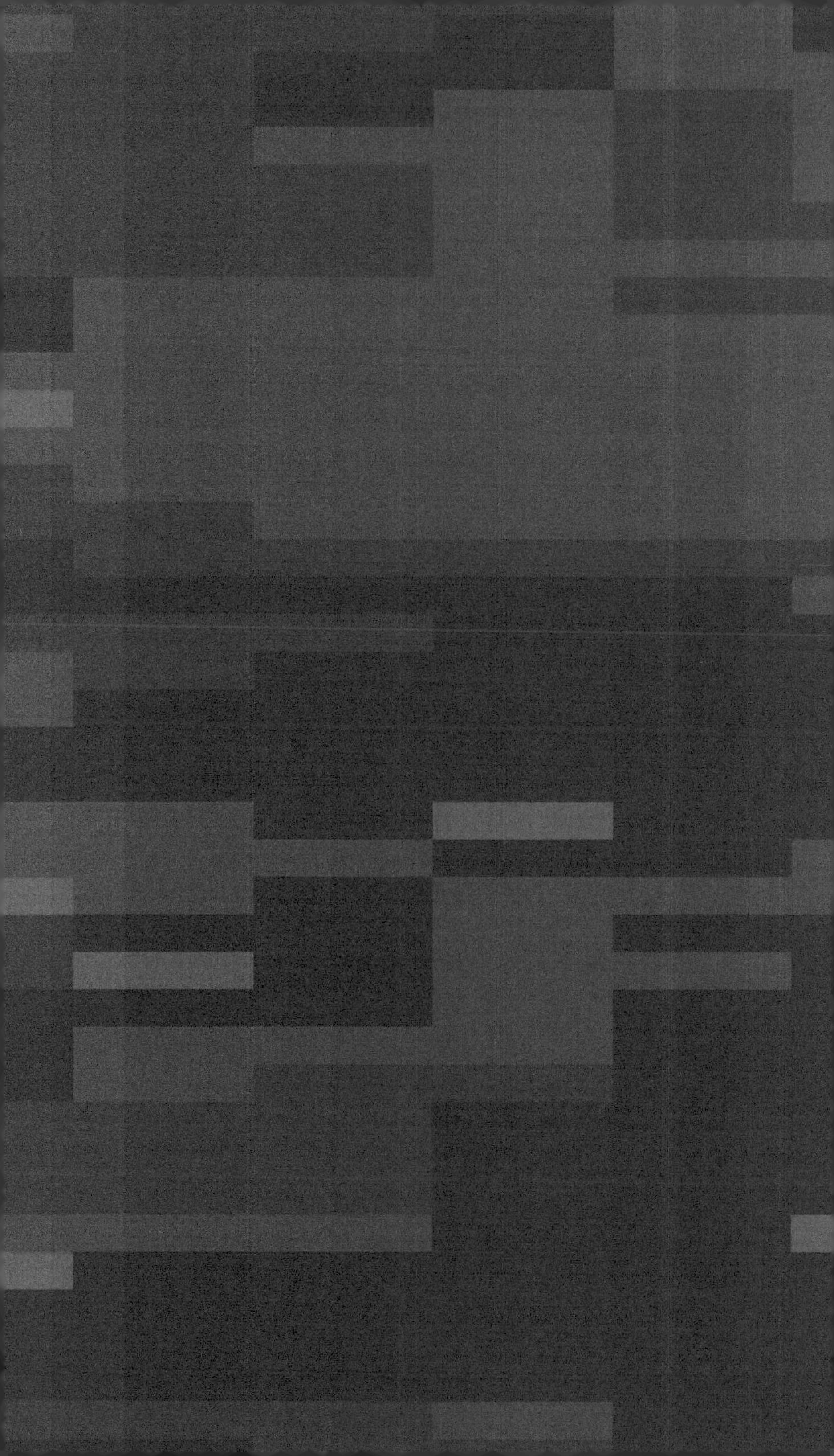

THE LAST LUNCH
[52:21:10]

There'd been a bit of something at Stratospherical, since both Stabbo and Serpentina were heavily wired up. The host, who was a black-suited, middle-aged man with white hair and mustache, reminded them of the strict no-kill policy on the premises, which made Stabbo laugh.

"This is a Yak establishment, yeah? Or Triad?" Stabbo asked, which embarrassed the host. Any mention of gang affiliations was the height of gaucherie, but a cyberclown could be impertinent at will, apparently.

"We are very well-protected, sir," the host said.

"Don't worry about it," Stabbo said. "I'm not going to bloody up the place."

Stratospherical was more of a disc than a sphere, being a slow-rotating pile of ballistic windows that offered patrons an amazing view of the clouds below, the sun and sky above, and all of the Upperton spindles piercing the skyline like manmade mountains. Hovercars flitted back and forth, coming and going, no doubt to self-important or even actually important places. The colors of the restaurant were red, gold, and white, with machine-loomed red and gold carpeting and red and gold booths.

"It must be lovely up here at night," Moxie said, as they were walked to one of the window booths. "Romantic, even."

Cam noted that the lunch attendance looked to be up, with Spiffs aplenty around them, doing their best to appear unimpressed, but watching all the while. He could see the eyes watching them, evaluating, assessing, judging, calculating, wagering.

"It certainly is," the host said. "We boast one of the best views in the city, regardless of the weather."

Everyone took their seats, Cam taking the time to study Stabbo, who seemed unbelievably at ease and even charming. How this man could be the fearful snuff apparition of infamy was hard to square. His in-person demeanor was unlike the leering face Cam had seen on their feeds, with strong features that radiated a military no-nonsense bearing touched with a bone-dry bemusement.

Stabbo ordered them a bottle of champagne and four glasses, looking at Cam from across the table. Their feeds looked strange, each one in each other's cybereyes. The audience was loving it, with so much chatter that Cam actually had to turn it down a bit to keep his eyes on Stabbo without being distracted.

"You're a good-looking guy, Cam," Stabbo said.

"Quite the Looker," Serpentina said, grinning toothily at him. Her voice was husky, beautifully breathy. Enough so that Cam wondered if she'd practiced at it or had gotten some elective surgery on her vocal chords to render it that way. Maybe a bit of both.

"Thanks," Cam said.

"I see why your peeps follow you," Stabbo said. "I'd watch this guy, wouldn't you, Tina?"

"Very closely," Serpentina said, looking him up and down, licking her lips, confirming the forked tongue, to Cam's quiet satisfaction.

"A shame you're set to kill him," Moxie said.

"Yeah, about that," Stabbo said. "You want to talk shop a little? We still have around fifty-two hours until *Lookout* wraps. You have any preferences around where you want to go? Up here? Down there? Midtown?"

"No preference," Cam said, trying to appear chill as the champagne was brought out. It was Dom Pérignon, an old-time brand that had come cachet in particular circles. The grapes for it were said to be grown in a clandestine climate-controlled location, guarded by multi-generational mercenaries and paramilitaries.

"You're a Midtown kid, so, I wasn't sure if you wanted to end up there," Stabbo said, watching the server pour. It was a young woman with carefully coiffed black hair and a prominent nose. She managed everyone's pour to perfection, before slipping away.

"Champagne for lunch," Moxie said, taking her glass. "How decadent are we?"

They raised their glasses, clinking them and taking their drinks.

"Midtown's as good as anywhere for me," Cam said, to Stabbo, while Moxie eagerly sipped her champagne. Despite her own ample wheeling and dealing, it was a level of opulence she had never had before, judging from her gleeful reaction.

"Although it might be nice to spill some blood in Uptown," Serpentina said, glancing around them, smirking at the other patrons. "Way too bloodless up here, if you ask me."

Stabbo fiddled with his glass as the server brought over crab cakes and some bowls of berries, which particularly delighted Moxie, who speculated on the origins of them, thinking maybe there might be greenhouses somewhere in Upperton, although Cam doubted anyone in Upperton would stoop to something as prosaic as agriculture.

Cam could see the fans were ogling big-time, their numbers climbing with the combination of the venue and, more importantly, the contenders facing one another across the table. Stabbo could see it, too.

"I think tomorrow could work," Stabbo said. "You picked this place. You can pick tomorrow's venue."

Of course, Cam didn't want to pick any venue. He didn't want to have to go up against this man—although "man" was hopelessly archaic and inadequate for what he was—"cyborg" was at least more accurate. There was something, too, which Cam was picking up. As a Looker, he was used to seeing more than others, and he was seeing something in Stabbo, a cocktail of thoughts and emotions that others wouldn't have noticed, but he sure did.

"You know what? We can let our agents work it out," Cam said.

"That's a great idea," Stabbo said. "Tina, you talk with Moxie later, work it all out."

"Will do, Stabs," Serpentina said.

"I'll set something up," Moxie said, tapping her monocle. Her own fingernails were painted a purple that nearly matched the berries.

"I have to ask," Cam said. "Why 'Stabbo' anyway?"

Stabbo smiled at him. No fangs; just straight, very white, perfect teeth.

"You know, stage name," he replied. "Every cyberclown has a stage name, you know? Bingo used to call us 'the Circus' and that just stuck."

"It's pretty weird," Cam said. "Just saying."

"We laugh so that we don't cry," Stabbo said.

"In cyberspace, everyone can see your tears," Cam said.

Stabbo found that amusing, laughed, drinking down his champagne and pouring some more. His movements were so smooth. Cam doubted he'd be able to even get a shot on him.

"Yeah, I get that," Stabbo said. "We just owned it. The Polygon made us all into freaks, and we took it as a kind of honorific. Nobody makes us anymore. Truth. They don't load up soldiers that way these days. They do full combat chassis work, with consciousness extraction. They do killbots and drones and take out the middleman. It's just cleaner that way, even if it's more expensive. Less trouble than welding flesh to chrome."

Cam didn't really know what he was talking about, but went along, anyway. The art of being a Looker involved paying attention and keeping things rolling, without getting hung up on anything in particular.

"Right now, I think the Polygoners are just waiting for us to die off," Stabbo said. "They have a special corps of Ghouls out there, waiting to scoop us up and recoup their investment."

"Do you know Polly Tryhard?" Moxie asked.

Stabbo laughed.

"Never had the pleasure," Stabbo said. "She's that high-value Valkyrie, yeah? She's a bit upscale for somebody like me."

"She's amazing," Moxie said. "Totally chrome."

Stabbo pondered that.

"I've thought about it," he said. "Just ditching the meat entirely and going fully chrome. Cost a fortune, and there's the adjustments, all of that. I don't know if I could do it. Crazy to think of it that way, from your perspective, I'm sure. But I don't know."

Cam thought the cyberclown was about as posthuman as a person could get. Or, at the very least, transhuman. The idea that there were still further steps on the path made him uneasy. His eyes had been a big step for him, but the rest of him was flesh-and-blood, besides the headware he'd gotten to accommodate the optical rig.

"What about you, Cam? What makes a guy ditch his own eyes for cybers?" Stabbo asked.

His own path felt far more baseline, less fraught than Stabbo's own soldier's journey. Cam had bad eyes and good looks, had made a deal with Oniyaki, who offered him a way up and out, for a price, of course. It had made sense at the time. He certainly wasn't going to just blurt that out while they were viewing each other.

"Young and dumb, man," Cam said. He glanced at Moxie, who looked back at him while she nibbled some crab cake and sipped champagne, pretending innocence. "Needed the money. Needed a way up and out of the gunk. Saw the opportunity and I took it."

"How're those Eyeconics working out for you, anyway?" Stabbo asked. "Was thinking I might score some myself, once this wraps up."

"They're great," Cam said. "Fully intuitive. The resolution is crazy."

"Yeah, I can see that," Stabbo said. "I look great through your eyes. Don't I, Tina?"

"Sure do, Stabs," Serpentina said.

They had used the table to order their lunches, which had a simplejack interface they all took advantage of. Stabbo had vat steak and quail eggs, while Serpentina had pork belly bao buns. Moxie opted for spicy garden sushi, and Cam had Japanese fried chicken with spiced honey sauce.

"I've never dined with somebody I was going to snuff," Stabbo said. "Kind of a trip, really."

"I'd say I've never dined with somebody out to kill me, but that'd be a lie," Cam said. "I seem to bring it out in people. Luck of the Looker."

They laughed at that, Cam pouring more champagne for the agents and then for himself, while Stabbo ordered another bottle brought over.

"It's true," Moxie said. "Everybody wants to kill Cam sooner or later."

"I had a crazed fan, once," Cam said, Moxie giggling nervously. "He went by the name of Welcome Matt. He was fixated on me. Followed me everywhere. Especially once he figured out where I lived. I mean, he'd stake me out and follow me anyplace I'd go."

"Creepy," Serpentina said. "What'd you do?"

"I worked it," Cam said. "I mean, it became like a game for people. Like I'd do my thing, my Looker thing, and peeps would try to spot Welcome Matt in the frame. This went on for about six months. Audience climbing, people watching me play cat-and-rat with Welcome Matt, wondering how it would play out. He calls me, writes me. He's obsessed with me. Dyes his hair like mine. I mean, he doesn't look like me, but he *wants* to look like me."

Cam went through his headware and shared some stills of Welcome Matt, his wild eyes looking like a parody of Cam, synthleather jacket and jeans.

"What a nutwad," Stabbo said. "So, what happened to the Plonker?"

"He got killed by some Triads," Cam said. "They thought he was me, spying on them. He was out trying to be me. He wore this headrig, like counterfeits of my shades, with a wraparound interface that let him record what he was seeing through his lenses. He wore a recorder strapped on his back. I mean, like pretending, play-acting. Whatever you want to call it. And some drugged-out Triads gunned him down when he'd witnessed something he wasn't supposed to."

"Poor Welcome Matt," Moxie said. "He died being who he loved."

"Yeah," Cam said. "They stole his rig, sold his body to the organ grinders. Nothing wasted. The Triad guys came to me and staged a meetup. They apologized for the misunderstanding. No harm, no foul."

"Nobody poses as us," Stabbo said. "I mean, the kooks, yeah. The street toughs and wannabes like you saw the day before. But nobody's fooled by that. Nobody *wants* to be us. Not really."

"Aww, the tragic cyberclown," Serpentina said, feigning a tear down her reptilian face with a long finger, as their lunch arrived. "Never let him fool you, Cam. He loves who and what he is, and what he does."

"Yeah," Stabbo said. "Never let me fool you, Cam."

The audience feed grew, people slavering over the sumptuous lunch, while the Stratospherical disc slowly turned. Cam made sure to periodically glance out so people who would never be allowed to trek there could see it. Part of the dance of being a Looker was knowing how to bring people in, let them see what needed to be seen.

Stabbo gonna kill Cam. Right across the table.

No way. It's just lunch.

Lunch with punch.

Cam's gonna kill Stabbo.

Ha.

Truth.

Agents gonna kill them both! Snake eyes and One-eyed Jane.

She got both eyes.

The Monocle, y'all.
She got both eyes, all I'm saying.
Squeamish, I call her. She's a Squeam Queen.
Squeam.
Stabbo speared his steak and eggs, amused.
"Cows went extinct, didn't they?" he asked. "What am I even eating?"
Cam shrugged.
"It said 'vat steak' so I'm guessing it's bred somewhere," Cam replied.
"Probably in a vat," Moxie said.
"I'm older than you, I remember stuff like that," Stabbo said. "When all the meat substitutes came out in force—Chicken Big, Vat Steak, Pork Pie and Fish Cake, all of that stuff. I think the cows all died out when people stopped eating them. A few boutique bovines are maybe all that's left."
"Wouldn't know about that," Cam said.
"I'm sure they're somewhere," Moxie said. "The cows, I mean."
"I don't think so," Stabbo said. "Wildfires and all of that. The substitutes were just too easy to produce. That's the moral of the story, man—you do your part, and then you're done. When you're done, you're done."
"Well done," Cam said, making Stabbo laugh as he forked some more, dousing it with a little bottle of hot sauce that he'd had the server bring.
"We're all meat," Stabbo said. "More or less."
"Gross," Serpentina said. "We're eating, Stabs. Come on."
"Sure, sure," Stabbo said.
Cam wanted to kill his feed, just talk to Stabbo directly, but knew that wasn't going to fly with the thrall collar around his neck. He could imagine Oniyaki thumbing the kill switch and his own head popping clean off.

So, he went ghostmode and texted Moxie.

Mox, something's up. Talk to Tina after this. Make arrangements.

Moxie glanced at him, nodding as she took a sip of champagne.

"There's a viewing deck one floor up," Cam said. "The Canopy, they call it."

Stabbo glanced past the bar, could see the golden corkscrew stairs that led up.

"We'll have to check it out after lunch," Stabbo said.

"We should split lunch," Cam said.

"No, no," Stabbo said. "I insist. You know, last meal. That kind of thing."

"Such a gentleman," Serpentina said, mocking, giving Cam a wanton wink as she said it.

"Come on," Cam said. "Halfsies."

Stabbo wouldn't hear of it.

"No, no," he said. "Honestly, least I could do."

Cam watched the cyberclown wave him off, seeing his hands, which were crisscrossed with cybernetic haptic lattices. His fabled fingerclaws were right there, looking like ordinary digits, but fully weaponized to allow him to kill with them as easily as breathing.

Stabbo had killed over one hundred targets in *Stabbo's Meatmarket*. All of them had been bad people, curiously enough, murderers themselves—whether psycho killers, rogue enforcers, half-mad street samurai, thrill killers, street rats, twitchy Ghouls, crazed cultists, biker butchers, roadkillers. Those kinds of folks. Cam cycled through his kill list, had seen the dossiers of all of them. They were all like that. Cam was something else entirely for him.

Was Stabbo feeling guilty?

IN THE BUBBLE
[51:05:30]

They settled up lunch and went up into the Canopy, the host reminding Stabbo yet again about the no-kill policy, and up they went, drinks in hand. The Canopy had a dotted ring of red-cushioned benches around it, offering an exquisite view of everything. It was really more of a great bubble of auto-tinted polycarb. The absence of trideo ads was bracing to Cam, since everything from Midtown and lower was festooned with ads. It was almost peaceful, meditative.

"They used to have a skywalk," Moxie said, consulting her monocle. "But too many people were committing suicide from it, just stepping over the railing and sliding right down the disc and splattering below. We're six hundred and eighty-one meters up."

Stabbo whistled.

"Yeah, I imagine folks had time to think about what they'd done when they went over that side," he said. "That's a long drop."

"We'd call them 'Upperton Omelets' where I came from," Serpentina said. "Like the people who used to come down from above."

Cam leaned against the dome, gazing out at the clouds and skyspires that loomed everywhere. This was a very different world up here. Streetside, everything was horizontal, back-and-forth constantly, dripping with holographic advertisements and trideo screens. Even in Midtown, it was largely lateral, with upscale ad equivalents everywhere.

In Upperton, verticality was everything. The ascent was all that mattered, and, by extension, the ever-present prospect of tumbling down. Cam had built his entire life on seeking out an upward trajectory. He couldn't imagine attaining it and throwing it all away.

"We'd call them 'Splattycakes' where I grew up," Cam said. "Sometimes you could make some scrip if you got to them before the Ghouls or cops did. Like scrip, chits, trinkets, salvage."

"Makes me sad for them," Moxie said. "So much to live for, so much to lose."

A drinkerdrone hovered up behind them, a golden ball with whispermode quad rotors and a camera eye. Upperton drones always had whispermode rotors, which let them purr instead of the more grating whine that accompanied Streetside drones, or the high all-biz buzz of Midtown drones. It amused Cam to think that drone manufacturers paid attention to the noise level of drones depending on the markets for which they were building them.

Anybody Streetside running into a quiet drone assumed the worst—likely that they were about to be snuffed or at the very best, being spied upon. And nobody in Upperton would tolerate a noisy drone. He could not imagine one in a world like this, where everything was quietly opulent.

"Would anyone like more drinks?" the drone asked.

"Bring us up another bottle of Dom, Jeeves," Stabbo said.

Cam knew the cyberclown had blood filtration that likely kept him sober, but he was certainly tipsy, as was Moxie, who got chattier and more philosophical with each glass.

"I'm a Rust Valley girl," Moxie said. "I grew up in the Shambles. I mean, before I got to Shytown and met up with Cam."

"The Shambles? Yick," Serpentina said. The Shambles was a post-industrial wasteland east of Shytown, went on forever, ending at the drowned East Coast. There was another class of people in the Shambles—the Scavvers, who tried to make a marginal living out of whatever they got their hands on. Shamblers rarely got out of there. Moxie's own journey was a story Cam knew well.

"I'm no Shambler," Moxie said. "If that's what you think. I made my own way, you know?"

"We know," Cam said. "Everybody's from somewhere, Mox."

"I once hunted a guy in the Shambles," Stabbo said. "Biker bruiser, gearhead named Mack Sackson. One of the Bagheads."

Everybody knew about the Bagheads. They were biker psychos who wore cloth bags on their heads and killed people in the Hinterlands. They were notorious predators outside the Sprawl, one tribe among thousands like them, out to make themselves scrip by any means necessary.

"Killer response from that one," Serpentina said. "Mack Sackson would put plastic bags on people's heads and suffocate them. That's really why they were called 'Bagheads'—their victims were always found like that. Mack Sackson was one of their big dogs until Stabbo came and carved him up."

"Yeah," Stabbo said. "Ah, memories. I'm forever on their hit list for that little caper. You hear that, Baggers? You want to try to bag Stabbo, I'm always game."

Stabbo made a finger pistol and pointed it at Cam, making him nervous. The audience ate it up, of course, with wagers rising.

Stabbo's not clownin'

No, he's not.
Cam's shuttered. End of line.
Plonker! Cam's got tricks.
Dead man.
Stabbo's not playing, Spliffs.

Moxie shuddered as the drone came back up with the bottle of champagne in its armature. Cam wondered if it was an autodrone or whether somebody was actually piloting it, as it flitted about, pouring without spilling a drop. If it was a person driving it, they had very steady hands, could be making real money doing rigwork elsewhere. Cam didn't know whether it was his Looker persona or Streetside habits that made him see everyone's capacity to hustle. Steady hands meant steady work, and recognizing talent often meant the difference between life and death in Shytown.

"You're a bounty hunter," Cam said, feeling the champagne more than he wanted to admit. "Right?"

"Yeah," Stabbo said. "Bills to pay, Cam. It was Tina's idea for me to make a stimsense feed of it. Show people how the biz rolls. Although I haven't run live until *Lookout.* Just because with the tossers I've chased down, the last thing you want to do is give them advanced warning. They can't see you coming. But people enjoy watching me do what I do via stim."

"Ah," Cam said. Stabbo's audience was very different from Cam's. Cam hadn't snuffed anybody. Why Oniyaki had even set this up made Cam angry. He was effectively leveraging Cam's greater audience and visibility against Stabbo's own rabid fanbase, in what was clearly a mismatch. Stabbo seemed smart, he had to have been able to see this.

The drinkerdrone hovered nearby, having filled everybody's drinks.

"We are high up," Serpentina said. "Way up there. I think I can feel the building swaying a little."

"I've never been in orbit," Moxie said, gazing skyward. "I hear it's amazing up there."

"Me, neither," Cam said. "The Heights, yeah. Super fancy. Top-notch."

"Overrated, if you ask me," Stabbo said. "But then again, they'd never let someone like me up there. I'd set off stationwide alarms. You know I can't even really travel except for private-like."

"Poor killer clown," Serpentina said, looking pretend-sad. "The walking weapon."

Stabbo smiled into his fluted glass, waved the drinker-drone over for a refill, watching it pour. Cam could see lines in the sky, being shuttles or spaceships going to unknown destinations. Anyone using private transport instead of the elevators had to be really slinging scrip, total bizzos. He knew he'd never ride that high. Lookers never lasted. It was something everybody knew. Sooner or later, they blinked and were wasted.

"Just saying," Stabbo said. "Fragistan was a long time ago. I feel obsolete."

"You're not obsolete," Serpentina said. "You're merely transitioning."

"Hey, not to be a twanker, here," Cam said. "But I'm the one whose life is on the line. Enough pity party for the cyberclown."

Stabbo laughed, clapping Cam's shoulder. Even a casual pat like that conveyed the man's strength. Cam was sure Stabbo could break him in half if he wanted to.

"You said it, Cam," Stabbo said. "You're the walking dead man. I forget sometimes."

Cam went ghostmode and sent something to Stabbo. It was a daring move, as he saw it, but his headware was secure, and he doubted anybody would dare to crawl in Stabbo's cranium uninvited.

Let's come to an arrangement.

We talking biz, now?

Yeah. It's why you set this lunch up, yeah?

Stabbo watched some hovercars flying over the clouds toward one of their skyrises, while Serpentina and Moxie talked. Anyone taking a hovercar this high was hardcore bizzo. It made Cam think of his ride to Oniyaki's lair.

I admit I did want to kill you. I mean, just another stupid Looker, right?

But?

You're alright. I see how you do what you do. I want more of that.

As I see it, we could bet on a draw.

Ha. My reputation would never recover.

Different audiences. None of the other clowns run stim feeds, yeah?

No, they don't. They're smart. They lay low. I play it loud on purpose. Can see the tossers and plonkers coming.

Moxie was telling Serpentina her philosophy of cybernetic enhancements while Stabbo and Cam ghostmoded each other. As a Looker, Cam was experienced with multitasking, holding casual conversations while sending ghost-texts to others in the field. The fly Lookers could do it without anyone being the wiser. Cam was sure Oniyaki had spies on nonstop to monitor their feeds.

"I am not against body mods," Moxie said. "But I'm not for them, either. Does that make sense?"

"No," Serpentina said. "You can't be value-neutral on mods. I mean, you're jacked, aren't you?"

So there it is. You run the table with the POV stimsense franchise. Lookout becomes your thing. Oniyaki's just using me to drive the audience there. He's banking that you killing me will drive up engagement.

Look at you go, begging your life like you're doing me a favor.

"I'm only minimally jacked," Moxie said, waving her champagne glass around. "Just basic data headware, headphone and slots, just to keep tabs on my clients. Can't leave'em lurching, you feel me?"

"Samewise. That's how it always starts," Serpentina said. "I first did my teeth, you know? First thing I did. I went to Fangsalot."

Oniyaki's using us both. Fuck him. I'm saying we could do better if we bet on other outcomes.

Betting against the Yaks is bad biz. Like slow-motion suicide. They remember everything. They have accountants.

The Yaks aren't nearly what they once were. You know that. This is Oniyaki's big play, trying to stick it to the Triads, the Bratva, and the Skindicate. He's trying to branch out. But if this goes south for him, he's screwed.

I don't see how that works.

He's making scrip-n-chits from audience engagement, has his hands in the betting, sure. But he's banking on the obvious outcome—you killing me. He's got no imagination. I'm saying we bet on another outcome, the long odds, the one nobody sees coming. We make money from that.

"Don't they cause problems?" Moxie asked. "You know…"

"Nah," Serpentina said, smiling toothily. "You'd be surprised. And before you ask, yeah, they're venomous. Actually, I have a polyloading system in place—several drugs, three different venoms. I'm ready for all occasions."

I like your spunk, Cam. So, how does it play out?

We run out the clock, but make it count. Make it look good. Put on a good show.

I don't see how that plays, exactly. I'm supposed to cut you up.

So we make it look good. I shoot at you, you evade. You catch up, you slash at me. I evade. We wind people up. We choreograph it.

Showmanship.

Yeah.

"What kind of drugs?" Moxie asked.

"Hallucinogens, narco, speed, downers, aphrodisiacs," Serpentina said. "I'm a walking pharmacy, depending on the sitch."

"Crazy," Moxie said. "How do you replenish them?"

Serpentina pointed to her mouth.

"Orally, obviously," she said. "You should get a pair."

"No way," Moxie said. "Fangs? I dunno."

"It helps," Serpentina said. "You have no idea how often they'd come through for me. And they're stronger than enamel. Way stronger. Do yourself a favor and consider them. Oh, and sweet thing that you are, you can get re-tractable. Me, I keep them out all the time, but the retractable is an option."

"Good points," Moxie said, running a tongue over her pristine teeth, while Serpentina looked on, smirking. "I might check that out."

Way ballsy to try to stick it to Oni.

Better payout. Longer odds.

Oni wants you dead. That's the thing.

Yeah. Not sure why. He killed Sandra Scene and Victor Glimpse.

Get outta here.

Truth. Told me as much. But, you know, I was Stoppered.

"Keeps guys on their toes, you know what I mean?" Serpentina asked.

"I can imagine," Moxie said. "I had my teeth done awhile ago, but nothing like that. Just routine cosmetic work."

"Shambler chic," Serpentina said.

"Ouch," Moxie said.

"Hey, I'm a Rustville girl, I get it," Serpentina said.

So, we let Mox and Tina work out the deets on their own. Off-camera, while you and I make it look good. Like real good. I'm thinking a Streetside chase scene. Get the eyes on us, watch the bets roll in. I just need to survive another fifty-one hours.

Assuming Oni doesn't stick it to you and blow your head off. You should get somebody to hack that thing off you.

I was thinking maybe you might do that. Those crazy claws of yours I keep hearing about.

Might blow us both up. Might tip off Oni.

Maybe. But if the feed keeps going, maybe he won't mind. Or maybe he will.

"What's with the monocle?" Serpentina asked.

"I like it," Moxie said.

"Obviously," Serpentina said.

"It's fully linked up," Moxie said. "Plus, I can go anywhere with it. I pass baseline scans. I have a little red leather case for it when I travel."

"Real leather?" Serpentina asked.

"You know it," Moxie said. "A gift from an appreciative client."

"Anyone I might know?" Serpentina asked.

"Oh, probably," Moxie said, leaving it at that, nursing her drink with languid orbits of her wrist.

We have to make it look good. You toy with me, I run. You catch me. I escape.

I'm not an actor, man.

I know it. Just do what you do, and don't kill me.

Let's say we pull this off, then what?

Oniyaki's got his show, you're his new star. I'm a footnote.

Sounds like you walk off, and I'm stuck with the Yak.

We're all stuck with the Yak. I need to tell Nimble about what I know. But I can't. Not while I'm on.

Sounds like that's for your agent to do.

Yeah. On her TDL.

You trust her?

I do. Can I trust you?

Stabbo didn't hesitate.

You can.

Didn't you warn me not to trust you?

I did.

Stabbo grinned at him, raising his glass. Cam joined him, and the drinkerdrone joined them, refilling both of their glasses.

"May the better one win," Stabbo said.

"I'll drink to that," Cam said.

CLOWNING AROUND
[39:38:37]

Cam told Moxie about his plan in ghostmode, and she brightened up, tipsy as she was after Stratospherical. They'd managed to get to his Midtown flat before the next storm rolled in, the rain beating the ballistic windows, while Moxie sorted herself out, looking up trideo ads for Fangsalot as cover while she did. Cam was amused, thinking of Moxie with a pair of fangs.

Okay, so I need to talk to Nimble, tell her what you told me. And I'll make arrangements with Serpentina. What'll you do in the meantime?

I'll survive. Work with me on this.

After drunkenly plotting and doing one another in Cam's flat, they'd slept off all the Upperton booze they'd drunk, waking up hours later, feeling rested, if not entirely refreshed. They fucked before the moon reluctantly rose behind captivating clouds that smothered it, to the prurient delight of Cam's insomniac audience.

Cam's gettin' busy, Spliffs.

Long nights and last rites.

Moxie's a hottie.

Man's going out with a bang, yo?

Cam's feed was blowing up with peeps talking about Stabbo putting on polyflage body armor, except for his open hands, showing off his claws.

From the feed, his claw hands were terrifying. His fingers seemed to recede, slipping back into hand housings, revealing curved spars of reticulated alloyed steel that moved curiously. Each blade was about six inches long, but responded to servos that moved within the hand, so they could bend.

Stabbo's got a killer handshake.

Cam's going to be sliced like Dermapork.

Those are sick digits, Spliffs.

Stabbo swiped at a metal pipe, cutting clean through it, which delighted the onlookers. His strength and speed, plus the sharpness of the fingerblades made him absolutely terrifying, which thrilled the audience.

Cam put on a black turtleneck and black jeans, as well as his tactical walkers, tying the laces tightly. The clothing was high-grade antiballistic fabric, which should help him against standard rounds, if they came his way. He slipped the shotgun over his shoulder and put his G91 in a shoulder holster. He then snagged a grey polyflage hooded ballistic raincoat, savoring the feel of it in his hands, knowing that would play well with the stimmers.

Moxie watched him from his bed, wrapped in a green blanket, her eyes big with fear that looked genuine to anyone who didn't know any better, which was everyone.

"Good luck, Cam," Moxie said.

"Thanks, Mox," Cam said. "Lock up after you go."

"Sure thing," she said, her eyes tearing up. Whether it was from genuine worry or Moxie just playing the part for the sake of their caper, Cam thought it played nicely, and he made sure to look at her closely so those tears showed up clearly on the resolution. He gave her a lingering kiss and she kissed him back.

Cam could see from the twin-track feed that Stabbo wasn't so far. He was lurking in the Pedway, waiting for him somewhere. It all amounted to trust, as Cam saw it. And making it count. That was critical.

It was raining harder than usual, thunderclaps and hefty splatters turning the street into a cathedral of light, from reflected puddles and the raindrops that caught every lick of neon that loomed all around them. Audience aplenty were tuning in.

Don't do it, Cam!

He'll kill you!

Stabbo don't play, Cam!

Cam cradled the shotgun. It was around midnight, a dangerous time to be out. Even though nobody slept much in Shytown, there weren't as many out this time of night, which Cam counted on.

He went down the wet stairs to the street, flitting on his hood and activating the polyflage, which went into its adaptive mode that was of limited use in the driving rain, since Cam simply looked like an apparition shrink-wrapped in acid raindrops, while trideo ads blinked and winked all around the skyrise manmade mountains of ballistic glass and flexsteel.

The plan was to play offense a bit in this round, to go looking for Stabbo. The cyberclown was perched like a gargoyle on a rooftop, was watching Cam approach, had him zeroed. It was unnerving to see himself targeted in Stabbo's eyes. His onlookers piped up, messaging in his feed, as did Stabbo's.

Stabbo's right there, Cam! Above you!

Clown about town.

Line of sight, Cam. Look up!

Quit clowning, Stabbo! Kill! Kill! Kill!

Kill him, Stabbo! Gouge that Looker's eyes out!

Cam let his eyes travel up, using the Eyeconics to zoom in. And there he was, using his own adaptive polyflage, a shimmering rooftop wraith.

He brought up the shotgun and fired a shot, a slug, the gun letting out a thundering blast that was blended with the din of the storm.

At that range, the slug missed its mark, dislodging some masonry to one side of Stabbo.

"Stupid far for that thing, Cam," Stabbo said, jumping from his perch to the rooftop overhead.

Cam yanked down the ancient fire escape and climbed his way up the rusting stairs, wondering how he'd possibly sell it. Stabbo was quicker, stronger, and far deadlier than he was. He had to let himself seem as desperate and hopefully dangerous as possible.

He huffed and puffed up the escape, while, on the parallel feed, Stabbo simply waited, amusing himself.

"I know right where you are, Kid," Stabbo said, calling him. "I'll let you fire another shot or two, because I'm a nice guy."

"Thanks," Cam said, grateful that the building was only five stories. "Think I can catch my breath at the top?"

"I'm generous, but not *that* generous," Stabbo said, watching Cam's cloaked self reach the top.

Cam raised and fired the auto shotgun right at Stabbo, who moved with inhuman swiftness to sidestep the fusillade, the variable shot types whizzing past Stabbo as he reached the ground. The POV of it was breathtaking, with the muzzle flashes of the shotgun punctuating each blurry step Stabbo took to evade them. Seeing the cyberclown move that way was incredible, and Cam was, despite his edginess, grateful to capture that footage of the man-monster in motion.

He ran in a curious manner like this, hunching forward, arms out, fingers splayed. Even cloaked, he looked fiendish.

Cam fired off shots at the approaching cyberclown, who disabled his polyflage to let Cam get a proper look at him, white-faced and leering, wearing some sort of boonie hat to keep the rain out of his eyes. The audience was losing it, flinging commentary like shurikens.

Face of death, Spliffs.

Chalkfaced goon!

Cam's dead.

Light's out, Looker.

FASTER, STABBO! KILL! KILL! KILL!

"Attaboy," Stabbo said, dodging shot after shot, the auto shotgun blasting away, tearing holes in the rooftop where Stabbo had been only moments before. "Going out with a bang-bang-bang."

The way he ate distance when he moved, it was astounding to Cam, who was able to track it with his Eyeconics, even if he was moving quicker than Cam could target-track.

Stabbo batted away the shotgun, which went clattering across the old rooftop.

"Kudos to Devilish for giving you that choice toy," Stabbo said, slashing at Cam with one of his clawed hands.

Their onlooker audience was five million and counting, as Cam yanked the G91 from his holster and fired off some shots at point blank range, the bullets sizzling past Stabbo, who seemed only mildly inconvenienced by the pistol fire.

Cam could imagine how the cyberclowns must have terrified the Fragistanis, for they moved so quickly as to barely seem to be flesh and blood at all.

Stabbo's left hand clamped down on Cam's gun arm, the claws snicking around his arm like cuffs. His strength and leverage were prodigious, and Cam could feel the force applied pointing his pistol away from Stabbo.

"Too easy, Kid," Stabbo said. "You're a lover, not a fighter."

Cam threw an elbow at Stabbo, catching him in the face which made his ocular feed skip a beat from the force of the blow, to the thrill of the onlookers.

"I like spirit," Stabbo said, slashing at Cam, who flinched as the blades came down. The flinch saved his life, the razorfingers cutting the thrall collar into four pieces, which Stabbo quickly snatched and flung away, even as the pieces detonated in bright flashes and deafening blasts.

The whole thing took place in fractions of a second, something that would be replayed later, showing how Stabbo had cut at Cam, missing his neck, catching the collar, splitting it, then grabbing the pieces and tossing them in a blurring moment that even on slowed-down replay went quickly. The pieces detonated like tiny fist-sized suns—enough explosive force to readily sever a head, but not much else. The thrall collar's last timestamp was indicated at detonation:

$$[39{:}03{:}02]$$

Cam set his own internal timeclock to continue a countdown for the continuity of the audience, and so Oniyaki wouldn't zing him on some sort of Yak technicality, like breach of extortion or something.

"Whoa," Stabbo said, momentarily jarred by the cluster of explosions, which Cam used to effect a tumbling retreat, slipping free from the cyberclown and firing shots from his G91, the bullets finding their mark on the ballistic armor Stabbo wore, knocking him back. Cam kept firing, the pistol shoving Stabbo back until he fell over the side, clattering down the fire escape.

Cam ran to pick up his shotgun, pocketing the pistol, running to the fire escape, but Stabbo was already gone.

"Fuck," Cam said, like he meant it, looking this way and that, trying to see where Stabbo had fled to. Stabbo's own feed had him directly below Cam, Streetside, looking up from the shadows, back in his cloaked mode.

"Nice one, Kid," Stabbo said. "Took the wind out of me, there, just a little. You gotta aim a little higher if you want to take me down."

Cam ran across the rooftop and looked for a spot to jump. There was another adjoining building, one that ran right against the one he was at, just lower by a floor. Cam went to it and climbed over the side, landing gingerly on the soaked rooftop.

Stabbo, in the meantime, was stalking his way back up the fire escape, running his claws along it, the scraping making a squeal of old metal against new. Cam's fans went up against Stabbo's on the feed:

Stabbo's on the roof, Cam!

Kill him, Stabbo!

Kill that pretty boy!

Shoot that damn clown down!

Cam kept running, mindful of his step, switching to thermographic, which turned everything to cool shades of blue, except for Stabbo, who was a rainbow of colors. As if in mockery, Stabbo went to thermographic with his own eyes, and Cam stood out in the rain as if he had been a walking flare.

"I see you, Looker," Stabbo said, jumping onto the roof as Cam ran across the next roof, a slanted old structure. Above them was the Midtown Pedway, alternately blocking the rain and flinging rivulets down via drainage ports. The various skyrises were foggily luminous in the mist and rain, great monoliths to commerce over the ages.

Cam fired off a couple of shots from his shotgun, wild shots, one of which nearly caught Stabbo, who laughed.

"Flechettes," Stabbo said. "Cute. Glad you got some bang for your buck, Cam."

Cam slid over the side of the building, down an antiquated ladder, which took him down into a narrow alley packed with detritus—old tires, broken bits of plastic and Styrofoam, things that either somebody hadn't been able to salvage or hadn't gotten around to salvaging, yet.

He emerged on the street, catching his breath, glancing back. Stabbo was just a bright smudge, while he was the same on Stabbo's own screen. Cam again took some satisfaction that his Eyeconics offered a sharper, crisper image than Stabbo's.

Stabbo retracted his claws, holding them in front of his eyes so the onlookers could see them fold back into themselves, becoming hands again. Then he began climbing down the ladder.

Cam thought about waiting for the clown to descend. From his perspective, the narrow alley was a perfect firing line for him. So, he waited while Stabbo descended.

Stabbo, it's a trap! Look out!

Cam's gunnin' for ya, Clown!

Shoot him, Cam! You got him!

Cam waited, his target-tracking zeroing in on Stabbo. He fired the auto shotgun as Stabbo approached, the cyberclown dodging and then hiding behind a dumpster as the shotgun pelted the thing, making it ring with each shot.

No, Cam! Don't just shoot!

You gotta close with him!

Get up close!

Stabbo's reelin'!

The dumpster was denting and getting pockmarked by the mix of rounds, the weapon roaring and steaming as the raindrops fell upon it. Then it clicked, Cam having emptied it.

Stabbo popped up, grinning at him from the far side of the dumpster.

"Click," Stabbo said.

He held out his left hand like he was doing a magic trick, and Cam saw it transform back into his dreadful clawed appendage, while he slung his shotgun and drew his G91.

Cam fired two shots, Stabbo's revved reflexes allowing him to dodge them both, his body blurring as he moved, with effortless ease.

"My turn, Funboy!" Stabbo said, running down the alley toward him. Cam fired three more shots, all of which Stabbo dodged, and then he decided to run away.

Cam ran into a trio of greasepainted goons, who hooted and hollered as they snagged him, Cam cursing as he tried to shoot them, only to be restrained.

"Yo, Stabbo! We got him!" one of them yelled. They wore see-through rain slickers with rain hats, their white faces ghostlike in the mix of neon and rain.

Stabbo sauntered up, cackling.

"Is this Audience Participation Night or what?" Stabbo asked.

"Get him, Stabbo," another of them yelled.

"Let him go, Plonks," Stabbo said.

"Kill him, Stabs!" the third one said, all teeth.

Stabbo wagged a blade finger at them.

"I said let him go," Stabbo said. "Unless you want to be on the menu."

They shoved Cam as they reluctantly released him, the three of them staring at Cam with murderous desire, while Stabbo smiled.

"Good kids," Stabbo said. "Now off with you. I've got stuff to do."

"You soft, Stabbo," one of them said, sullenly. Stabbo slashed at him with an index finger, the blade cutting right through his slicker and boiler suit, across his chest, from which blood sprayed. The sullen one let out a cry of dismay, his white-gloved hand going to his chest, which was quickly covered in blood and raindrops.

"Who else wants an autograph?" Stabbo asked, wiggling his fingerblades. The other two grabbed their wounded friend and took off running, leaving a trail of blood behind them.

"That's going to scar," Cam said.

"Count on it," Stabbo said. "Now, where were we?"

Cam pointed the G91 at Stabbo, who laughed.

"One hundred thousand says you miss," Stabbo said.

"At this range?" Cam asked.

"Hell, yeah," Stabbo said.

The onlookers were now climbing toward six million. The audience was spellbound, which made Cam think they were selling it.

"Alright," Cam said, pulling the trigger.

SPEEDING TOWARD ELYSIUM
[29:19:09]

The G91 did its job, the bullet fired and flew at Stabbo, who stepped right out of its way, the bullet only creasing his right ear, just the hint of a cavitating lesion across the side of Stabbo's head, his reflexes amazing to behold.

From his own feed, the bullet looked like it moved almost in slow motion, like an inconvenience to be avoided. Cam wondered why Stabbo even allowed the bullet to touch him at all. Maybe the bit of blood from it was him trying to make it feel more real.

"Damn," Stabbo said.

"You owe me 100K," Cam said.

Whatever drove him to do it, his next move was to use his left clawhand to slice Cam's G91 in half, leaving only the grip and trigger guard gleaming in the Looker's hand. Cam thrust at Stabbo with that, like a half-assed brass knuckles while Stabbo grabbed him with his right hand, giving him a fling that sent Cam tumbling onto the street. Cam tossed the ruined G91 back at Stabbo, who only laughed.

"Dyin' time's here, Cam," Stabbo said, raising his clawed hand, as Cam got to his feet. All at once, a yellow Dodge Devastator with a black racing stripe and a reinforced black roll bar across the front roared onto the sidewalk and caught Stabbo in the chest, sending the cyberclown flying back, splashily somersaulting a dozen meters away.

Nimble peered at Cam from behind the steering wheel.

"Get in here, Cam," Nimble said. "Like now, Slowpoke."

Cam ran to the passenger side and threw himself in, while Stabbo was getting to his feet, cracking his neck with a turn of his head.

"What, Shytown PD watching the show or what?" Cam asked. Nimble gave him a saucy smile.

"Oh, you know it," Nimble said. "The bets are flying fast and furious on the force."

"So much for law and order," Cam said.

"We show up when we're needed, Looker," she replied. Nimble then threw the Devastator into reverse as Stabbo began running for them.

"There's a pistol in the glovebox," Nimble said. "If you're so inclined."

She whipped the car around, in a fishtailing spin, before throwing it into first and getting them out of there. Stabbo ran with them for half a city block before giving up the chase. He dialed up Cam.

"I'll see you soon, Looker, promise," Stabbo said, waving with his clawed hand a moment before he retracted it.

Nimble put a blue flasher on her dash as she cut through the city.

"You got yourself in trouble, looks like," Nimble said.

"Yeah," Cam said.

"Stupid, you know?" Nimble said. "Stabbo's a killer."

"Not really my choice," Cam said. "Hard to explain."

"Couple of white guys trying to kill each other? Try me," Nimble said.

He went to ghostmode.

Moxie talked to you, yeah?

Yeah.

She tell you what I saw?

Yeah.

And?

Oniyaki's a hard target. All but off-limits.

Can't you do anything?

Oh, I can, but nothing legal.

Legal. Hah.

"I just need to get someplace safe," Cam said. "For another day. I just need to last another day."

He opened the glovebox and saw the Fossett .457 magnum revolver in there. It was the older sibling of the Fossett automatic that Nimble carried.

"That's Handbreaker," Nimble said. "She might get Stabbo's attention. Depends what kind of ballistic armor he's sporting."

"His skin's bulletproof, too," Cam said. "Or maybe only bullet-resistant."

"Yeah," Nimble said.

Cam looked over the large-frame revolver.

"She's an eight-shot," Nimble said. "Ecumenical in her smartgun associations. Lucky for you, she likes you."

Cam could see that Nimble had rendered some programming with Handbreaker that accepted his biosignature.

"Too kind," Cam said.

"One of my failings," Nimble said.

"I'm not technically permitted to have police protection. Rules of the game," Cam said. Nimble smiled out at the zipping cityscape, wiper blades flicking rain out of her way, the ads a torrent of color and motion, of people, places, and things, all promises offered without shame or reservation.

"I'm only protecting and serving," Nimble said. "I'd have done that for any Spliff I saw being chased by a killer clown."

Moxie tell you about the Stopper?

Yeah. Too bad. Not evidence.

How are you going to play it?

Still working on it.

He killed Sandra and Victor. Made it look like the Triads. Moxie told me.

That should count for something.

Somehow I think you don't want to end up entangled in this. Can't see that sort of courtroom drama working with your audience.

Nope.

Courts were another thing entirely, operating in a realm Cam studiously avoided. Judges operated with their own bodyguards and police forces in the form of marshals, who were empowered to carry out the judge's will. Most of the judges were in the pockets of various megacorps and adjudicated based on those associations. Anyone who was put before a judge without a mountain of scrip behind them would be buried, sometimes literally.

"How about the Hotel Elysium?" Cam said.

"Fancy," Nimble said. "You're always so flash, Cam."

"What can I say? Upscale is my baseline," Cam said, making Nimble smile as he used his headware to set up the reservation with a concealed carry waiver contingent on him committing to not using it on the premises without express consent of the building management.

I'm going to get that bastard, Oniyaki.

I'll help you, but it's going to take time. Right now, let Stabbo and me pick his pockets.

That what you're doing? You trust that psycho?

Kindasorta, yeah.

Cuz he looked like he was going to stick you with those pitchfork fingers of his.

Pitchfork? What's that?

Never mind.

We had to make it look real.

It looked real to me.

Cam took some professional satisfaction in that.

The Elysium's white neon unicorn against a purple crescent looked like home to Cam. The pride of Midtown, it offered Cam a measure of comfort and convenience that would at least give him a respite.

The audience approved, jumping in with comments on his feed:

Elysium. Fancy boy.

Stabbo's going to kill Cam in the Unicorn Lounge.

Oh, for realz.

Heard they had a real unicorn in the lobby.

Shuddup, Plonker.

Nimble drove to the Streetside carport, where Elysium personnel in purple and white livery were on-watch and on-guard, numbering a half-dozen plus a pair of autogun turrets and a hospitality drone somebody was driving somewhere.

"Be careful in there, Cam," Nimble said.

"Plan to," Cam said.

"Leave the shotgun," Nimble said. "We'll swap later."

We'll be in touch soon.

Yeah, we will.

Cam stepped out, slipping Handbreaker into his smart holster, feeling it shift to accommodate the revolver, which had a roughly ten-centimeter barrel.

"Mr. Sexton," the body armored doorman said, smiling in his finery, the Elysium unicorn logo emblazoned on his chest. The other hotel personnel were also looking sharp in the company colors, all of them heavily armed. Cam imagined they weren't fond of the street detail. The hotel kept its Streetside entrance open to accommodate limos and other guests using vehicles.

Cam watched Nimble drive off, away from the golden lights of the Elysium, off into the rainy darkness. He immediately felt less safe with her gone, despite the security presence of the hotel staff. He knew they wouldn't do a thing for him off of the hotel campus. His headphone rang in ghostmode, on an encrypted line. Oniyaki, Cam was certain. He answered.

What was that, Cam? You playing me?

Not me.

A cop? You bring a cop into your mix?

She just gave me a ride.

No cops. The rules. And you think it's cute that you lost your thrall collar?

It saved my neck. He'd have had my head but for that.

Convenient.

Lucky Looker, that's me.

Too lucky by half. Stabbo's playing with his food. Don't try to be clever, Cam. You don't have the practice.

Oniyaki hung up, leaving Cam sweating. He feared having some Yak thugs show up to reattach a replacement thrall collar. He privately vowed that he'd die before that happened.

The armored elevator door opened, and the hotel staff walked Cam to it. Inside, it was the same golden light, with golden doors that were emblazoned with the unicorn standard, while dark panes of obsidian polished to a mirror shine cast Cam's reflection back at him.

The elevator got Cam to the lobby, which opened, letting in a Midtown couple of Stiffs, a he and she power couple in black power suits, the man with pink hair, the woman with blue. They looked at Cam a moment down the ends of their precision-cut noses.

"You're that Looker, aren't you?" the woman asked.

"That's me," Cam said.

"The one being chased by the clown," the man said.

"The very one," Cam said.

They looked at one another, sharing a smile.

"We don't watch," the woman said. "Stimsense stuff like that's for twankers."

Cam nodded. Some folks turned their noses up at stimsense and trideo, which he thought was ridiculous, given that it was absolutely everywhere. Anybody who thought they could tune out the world was dreaming.

The audience didn't like that one bit:

Couple of Stiffs.

They're the twankers.

You should shoot them, Cam.

They look like each other.

Creeps.

The splitscreen showed Stabbo having acquired a motorcycle, was racing toward Elysium, thrilling his own audience with the whirring view as he zigzagged through traffic, rocking it with those fired-up reflexes of his. The speed he traveled was dizzying, and plenty of audience were drugging up while the glowing city blew past them in lines of light and color.

Cam watched the power couple get off on the 29th floor, while he rode to the 52nd, getting out and stretching. He'd not run like that in a long time. Not since he'd been a wannabe, doing whatever he could to conjure up some bric-a-brac scrip.

He keyed to his room and tossed his coat on a hanger, was going to order room service when he realized he wasn't alone in the room.

"Hello, Cam," Abby said, silhouetted against the city lights, wearing a facemask, resting her hand on her katana.

THERE AND YAK AGAIN
[28:41:13]

Cam considered drawing Handbreaker, but Abby only said "Don't" in a quiet voice that stayed his hand. She held up the Stopper. She was wearing shiny black leather body armor like a ballistic catsuit, and the shiny facemask only exposed her dark eyes.

"A peace offering," she said.

"No way," Cam said. "I'm not putting that thing on again."

"So, cut your feed," Abby said. "And I won't plug you."

Cam cut his feed, knowing better than to try to argue the point with someone like Abby. She didn't bother turning on the lights because they could both see in the dark—Cam using his low-light vision, and Abby with whatever natural abilities she'd been given when they made her.

"You and that clown think you're pretty smart, don't you?" Abby asked, standing up, approaching him. The way she moved was frighteningly steady, almost dancerlike.

"What are you talking about?" Cam asked, wanting to move away from her, but knowing she'd be on him before he could get anywhere.

"Please," Abby said. "The cutting of the thrall collar was a cute move."

"I don't like having a bomb around my neck," Cam said.

Abby moved close to him, looking up at him.

"No, I can imagine that would be uncomfortable," Abby said. Cam could see that Stabbo had arrived at Elysium, which was triggering alarms from the security personnel, who were scrambling to stop him from entering.

"What do you want, Abs?" Cam asked, trying to keep it casual. "What does your boss want now?"

"He's *your* boss, too," Abby said. "Don't forget that. He's been tracking the betting pools, seeing which way people are going. There's a draw scenario that's appeared, and he's wondering how that might have happened. It started after you lost your thrall collar. Oniyaki's smart, Cam. He knows you'd do anything to survive. It might've occurred to you to work some sort of deal with that clown out there. A compromise."

"That's crazy," Cam said. She was organic and didn't have access to the feed. She didn't know Stabbo was even now making his way into Elysium. Stabbo was on his best behavior, evading the hotel guards rather than killing them. His speed let him bypass them quickly, while they shot at him, trying to track him. Even the autoguns were having a hard time with him.

Her phone chirped, and she brought it up to her ear.

"Yeah?" she said. "Understood."

She grabbed Cam, her enhanced musculature making short work of him, shoving him back into the hallway.

"What's he doing, Cam? Is he rescuing you?" Abby asked.

"I don't know," Cam said. "None of what you're saying is making any sense."

"One of you is going to die," Abby said. "One or the other, Cam. Oniyaki's made that very clear."

"Why?" Cam asked.

"Audience, Cam," Abby said. "I don't even watch and I know that. Let's go to the deck."

"It's raining, Abs," Cam said.

Stabbo had managed to incapacitate the hotel security and was making his way up the elevator, which he jacked into in order to bypass its lockdown security protocols. Not wanting to disturb the other guests, the Elysium didn't sound a general alarm.

Abby walked Cam to the elevator bank and pushed the button.

"You two think you can screw with Oniyaki and live?" Abby asked. "That's arrogant of you. But I suppose that arrogance goes with being a Looker, yes?"

The elevator appeared and Abby walked Cam in, hitting the Deck button with an elbow. Cam's splitscreen showed only Stabbo's POV, and he was taking his own elevator up. Cam quietly flicked on his feed, letting his eyes rake over the elevator buttons, over Abby, showing where he was, who he was with, and where he was going.

Abby was oblivious, being only organic, after all.

The elevator opened to the Elysian Skydeck, which offered only a commanding view of Downertown, but for the locals, the sea of lights, trideo ads, and skyrises counted as a memorable view they'd have to pay dearly to afford. What the Elysium offered was a prime location, abundant services, and a level of security and protection that was worth the price.

There were gold and purple weatherproof tarps that offered protection for anyone choosing to venture out onto the wood-planked deck, where low tables had been set around firepits and crescent-shaped cushioned benches screened by carefully pruned fragrant trees that offered both privacy and a scent that camouflaged the stink of the city.

While it was in Midtown, the Pedway only went to the lobby area. The Deck was only accessible through the lobby. Or, Cam observed, if some commandos rappelled down from neighboring skyrises. But he bet the Elysium had countermeasures for that as well. Hotel security was formidable in Shytown, despite the short work Stabbo had made of the Streetside Elysians.

"Am I just supposed to let Oniyaki put my head in a noose?" Cam asked.

"More or less," Abby said, flicking her katana from her scabbard. She was scanning the deck for Stabbo, her phone ringing. She went to answer, but Cam snatched it, tossing it over the side. Abby rewarded him with a static-inducing backhanded smack that sent Cam flying.

The Deck patrons present, which looked to be two groups of Stiffs around two different firepits, gaped at them.

Abby watch Cam get up, smiling to herself.

"Please, Cam," Abby said. "There's more dignity in simply jumping over the side."

Cam drew Handbreaker and fired a shot at Abby, who dodged it deftly even as the Stiffs let out terrified screams. Living up to its name, Cam felt his hand throb from firing the shot, since it appeared there wasn't recoil compensation on Handbreaker. Nimble hadn't lied.

Cam up against that ninjalady.

With that katana, I bet that's Abby Normal.

She's a stone killer.

Yak Attack.

Yak? You sure?

What I just say, Twanker?

Abby ran at Cam with her katana, moving with a lethal, liquid grace as she cut the rain and air with her slender frame and the protected steel of the blade.

Cam fired a second shot from Handbreaker, the Fossett blasting a special shot bullet that sent a scatter of high-velocity shot at the assassin, who, despite her speed, was struck by the pellets, which threw off her attack, her katana biting not into Cam's shoulder, but into one of the sculpted hedges just past him.

Three purple-and-white hotel security drones flitted down, shining bright lights on them.

"You are in violation of the Hotel Elysium's hospitality protocols," one of the drones said. "Please put down your weapons immediately and lay on the ground."

"Dammit," Abby said, cursing, the spatter of blood across her chest and shoulder. "Who puts polyshot in a revolver?"

Bless you, Nimble, Cam thought, firing another shot at Abby, who threw herself to one side for cover, while the polyshot shell tore into one of the purple cushions. Cam did a mental note that he'd fired three shots. That gave him five more shots with the revolver.

Cam saw blood on the ground, pelted by the rain, as the elevator opened, and Stabbo emerged.

"Cease fire or we will shoot," one of the drones said. Cam assumed they were not autodrones, that there were pilots somewhere in the Elysium tending to them. The drones appeared to be armed with flechette guns, which made sense for the venue, since discretion was always the hallmark of Midtown hospitality.

Abby drew some throwing spikes from her catsuit and flung them at the drones with deadly accuracy, the spikes sticking into the metal of the drones and detonating on impact, turning all three of the drones into smallish fireballs, raining parts across the deck and terrifying the Stiffs.

"Cam? You still alive?" Stabbo asked.

"You know I am," Cam said.

Stabbo chuckled, while Abby cursed from the shadows.

"You two idiots are ruining everything," Abby said, dragging her katana along the deck, the blade scraping agreeably against the wood, the steel singing. Stabbo flicked up his hands, turning both of them into a cluster of blades.

"My kind of fight," Stabbo said.

The petrified patrons watched from their respective firepits as Abby emerged, holding her katana in both hands, blood running down one arm from where Handbreaker had nicked her.

"You die first, Clown," Abby said. "Then the Looker."

Cam watched the wagers flying across his feed, as people guessed that Abby would kill the both of them. He bet against her, bet for themselves, wondered what the hell Oniyaki was even thinking in all of this.

It was an uncanny confrontation—Abby was pure Yakuza organic, while Stabbo was entirely milspec cybernetic. Flesh versus chrome. East versus West.

They moved so quickly, and if Cam didn't have his Eyeconics, he might have blinked and missed it, but he didn't have to blink, and tracked it as Abby ran for him, swinging with her katana, which Stabbo caught and blocked, throwing a punishing kick to her midsection that sent her tumbling backward. He sprang for her, arms out in his strange, loping fighting stance.

She recovered from his kick, slashing him across his stomach with her katana, her blade biting past his body armor and into his ballistic skin, finding blood past the built-in protection as she cut. Stabbo let out a gasp and hacked at her with one of his hands, the fingerblades cutting deep on her already-wounded arm.

It was Abby's turn to throw a kick at Stabbo, right in the spot where she'd cut him, and the cyberclown grunted as he flew back from the force of her blow.

Cam had a clear shot, and took it, firing two shots with Handbreaker, not caring that his hand was numbing from the force of the pistol. But he was too slow, the shots sparking as they buried themselves into the deck where Abby had been only moments before. Even with his fast-tracking, she moved too quickly.

Abby stacked.

Stabbo hacked.

Cam whacked.

Can't shoot for shit.

Easier said than done, Spliffs.

Audience was surging past seven million, now, as the unexpected appearance of Abby Normal had charged up the word-of-mouth. Cam could feel the eyes on them as the fight continued. Hotel security was reengaging, judging from the feed, and onlooker accounts of an Elysian Unicorn Hospitality Strike Team assembling in the depths of the hotel, marching toward the elevators with paid-for purpose.

Stabbo recovered himself, one hand clutching his bleeding stomach, the other hand out to block Abby's katana blows, which came down in whirling strikes that would have killed anyone else. But Stabbo was fast and he was skilled, and he deflected each time, his own fingerblades holding their own against her katana.

Cam had three shots left with Handbreaker, and he took another one as Abby had raised her katana to bring down on Stabbo. The Fossett polyshot caught her in the chest, blowing her back, taking her to the edge of the deck, wheezing.

"Lucky shot, Cam," Abby said, blood on her lips, staining her facemask. Her black leather armor was shredded from the Fossett. While she'd been prepared for ballistics, the magnum propelled the shot, doing damage.

Stabbo lunged at her, hands out, sinking them up to his palms into her shoulders, the blades biting deep. Abby cursed, kneeing Stabbo hard in his open wound, then headbutting him, Stabbo crying out as he was knocked clear of her by the force of her counterattack.

Two shots left, Cam thought, taking them both, while Abby's attention was focused on Stabbo, who was momentarily down. Cam's target-tracking did its job, and both shots found their mark, the force of the magnum loads sending Abby flipping backward over the side of the Elysian Deck, her katana dropping near Stabbo's head, the blade biting deep into the wood.

Abby didn't even let out a scream as she fell, as the Elysian Unicorn Hospitality Strike Team came running out onto the deck in a cavalcade of branded body armor and flechette weaponry.

EVEN/ODDS & ENDS
[00:00:00]

The timeclock eventually ran out with a draw between Cam and Stabbo, to the mutual jubilation of their respective fan bases. Stabbo's MedEvac Gold Standard contract kicked in after Abby had cut him, with his MedEvac team flying in on a Quadraptor that whisked him away in a tense armed standoff between them and the Hotel Elysium Unicorn Hospitality Strike Team, who had sought to apprehend the cyberclown, only to be held back by the MedEvac Quadraptor that turned up, training its heavy guns on the Elysians while their paramilitary paramedics emerged in full white body armor with red crosses on their chests, snatching up Stabbo on a stretcher and strapping him in while the others covered with autoguns and drones forming a security perimeter.

Cam caught it all with his Eyeconics, Stabbo grinning bloodily at him, giving him a thumb's up with his own hands, the fingerblades tucked back inside him.

Watching Stabbo fly off in that Quadraptor, Cam almost wished he'd been wounded as well. Instead, he was forced to talk his way out of the fight on the deck with the Elysian hotel management, who pointed out his clear violation of his hotel agreement.

It was only because he was a Looker in the middle of a broadcast that they didn't lock him away. As such, since none of the patrons had been more than frightened by the battle on the deck, Cam was let off with a lifetime ban from the Hotel Elysium, and a bill for the destroyed drones and deck furniture, even though Cam pointed out that Abby had been the one who'd done most of that, not him.

That disappointing news was offset by the winnings Cam and Stabbo had garnered by betting on themselves and the outcomes they'd planned for. It earned Cam a cool two million chits, and at least a million for Moxie, who had hedged her bets, somewhat discreetly. Her fanged grin was catlike.

"What do you think, Cam?" Moxie asked, her tongue toying with her teeth.

"They suit you, Mox," Cam said. "Can't wait to see them in person."

"I'll bet," Moxie replied. "Try not to get killed in the meantime, Cam."

They ended their call with a scheduled meetup at the Plastic Fantastic, which would count as a victory lap, as far as Cam was concerned.

Oniyaki had cleaned up from the inaugural episode of *Lookout,* both in terms of audience clicks and his percentage of the revenue accrued from the shifting wagers, earning him at least twenty million chits from the accumulated wagering and clicks and replay residuals. It was almost enough for him to almost forgive Cam for his machinations. He'd sent men to gather Cam, Stoppering him and otherwise rendering him incommunicado.

"You must think you're pretty smart, Cam," Oniyaki said, drinking his tea, while Cam was made to sit and listen. "You and the Clown."

"I'd never cross you, Oniyaki," Cam said. He'd even brought back Abby's katana as a token of good faith.

The Yakuza lord only smiled at him, not believing a word of it.

"I knew you'd draw eyes, Cam," Oniyaki said. "I knew you would. It's what you do. You and the Clown."

Stabbo was recovering in the top-drawer MedEvac facility he'd been whisked to, somewhere in Chillwaukee. He'd gotten his ballistic washboard stomach replaced, and with enough pints of blood provided, was nearly as good as new.

"Glad I could help," Cam said.

"Sure you are," Oniyaki said. "You're lucky I'm a forgiving man. I have my new show. Not you and the Clown again, no worry. Others, though. Lucky souls. Maybe not as enterprising as yourself."

Cam hoped that Nimble would bring this man to justice but didn't know quite how she'd do it. He just drank his tea, kept his expression neutral. That was how one survived Oniyaki.

"We're not done, Cam," Oniyaki said. "Just so you understand this. We'll see each other again. And sooner than you might think."

With that, Abby appeared, joining them after clearing a shoji screen. Oniyaki seemed to delight in the stunned look Cam had on his face.

"Plenty more where she came from," Oniyaki said. "I assure you."

Abby took her spot to one side, her face carrying not a trace of emotion or recognition. Cam wondered if she knew what happened to her predecessor. He saw her eyes flit over the katana on his low table and saw her glance at him without expression.

"She knows what happened to her," Oniyaki said. "Thanks to your feed, ironically enough. Now go, Cam. We'll see each other again soon."

The new Abby walked toward him, and Cam got up, bowing to Oniyaki, afraid that this moment would be his last. But it wasn't.

"Time for you to go, Gaijin," Abby said, taking up the katana, which she slipped over her back.

"Okay," Cam said, as she walked him out of the room, carefully closing the shoji screen behind them. "I didn't realize you were a clone."

"You *should* have," Abby said. "It only makes sense."

"Does it?"

"It does to me," Abby said. "I saw the feed. Your feed. The Clown's feed."

"And?"

"Lucky shot," Abby said. "You won't get that again. I can promise you that."

"Nothing personal," Cam said.

"Nothing ever is," Abby said, walking him to the flying limo. Cam put on his shoes in the security area, while Abby was given Handbreaker and put on her own shoes. "Oniyaki told me not to kill you. So, there's that."

"I'll take that," Cam said. "For me, that counts as a win."

They stepped into the limo together, the blinkered Looker and the cloned assassin, each one assessing the other.

"Where to, Gaijin?" Abby asked.

Cam considered a moment, while the sun was setting somewhere, turning the clouds to a sea of glowing saffron and plum. Up here, higher than the sky, the troubles of the world seemed so far away. It was easy to get lost in Upperton, but Cam knew his new eyes would help him find his way.

"How about drinks at the Plastic Fantastic? My treat," Cam said. Cam wondered how many Abby clones there were. Knowing Oniyaki, there were probably hundreds of Abby Normals on-tap, ready whenever he needed them. He wished he could get a few clones of himself, too. Maybe one day, if he played it right. The world could use more of him, as he saw it. He watched the unseen sun smothering beneath the now bruise-purple clouds with his very expensive eyes.

"You *still* can't afford me," Abby said, arching an immaculate eyebrow at him.

"No?" Cam said, grinning. "Well, we'll see."

WHEN IN CHROME

BOOK TWO OF
THE PLASTIC FANTASTIC

COMING SOON!

A NOTE ON THE TYPE

The text of this book is set in Minion 3, an updated and expanded version of Robert Slimbach's iconic text typeface. The first version of Minion was released in 1990 and is inspired by classical, old style typefaces of the late Renaissance, a period of elegant, beautiful, and highly readable type designs. Minion Pro combines the aesthetic and functional qualities that make text type highly readable with the versatility of OpenType digital technology, yielding unprecedented flexibility and typographic control, whether for lengthy text or display settings.

Robert Slimbach, who joined Adobe in 1987, began working seriously on type and calligraphy four years earlier in the type drawing department of Autologic in Newbury Park, California. Since then, he has concentrated primarily on designing text faces for digital technology, drawing inspiration from classical sources. In 1991, he received the Prix Charles Peignot from Association Typographique Internationale for excellence in type design. Slimbach now directs Adobe's type design program.

The chapter titles of this book are set in Eurostile Extended, by Aldo Novarese for URW Type Foundry. The Eurostile font family was designed (by Novarese and Butti in 1952) to complement the titling font, Microgramma, by offering a lowercase alphabet. Issued by the Nebiolo foundry, the rather square sans serif Eurostile became popular for display and advertising use. The linear nature of Eurostile suggests modern architecture, and its attraction is technical and functional. Eurostile is commonly misspelled Eurostyle.

Composed by Clever Crow Consulting and Design
Pittsburgh, Pennsylvania

ACKNOWLEDGMENTS

I would like to thank Christine Marie Scott of Clever
Crow Consulting and Design in Pittsburgh for her won-
derful cover art and her invaluable assistance with the lay-
out and design of these pages.

ABOUT THE AUTHOR

Dean Vale lives and breathes Science Fiction at all
hours in an early 20th-century brownstone, where he con-
jures up progressively more dystopian and utopian visions
for the future of humankind. He is the author of *Farther*,
and *The Charge of the Wolverhino*.

FOLK HORROR & THE OCCULT

THE FIENDS IN THE FURROWS
Edited by David T. Neal & Christine M. Scott

The Fiends in the Furrows: An Anthology of Folk Horror
The Fiends in the Furrows II: More Tales of Folk Horror
The Fiends in the Furrows III: Final Harvest

THE CURSED EARTH, D.T. Neal

GRIMOIRE OF THE FOUR IMPOSTORS, Coy Hall

SONG OF THE RED SQUIRE, C.W. Blackwell

THE PROMISE OF PLAGUE WOLVES, Coy Hall

———

WEIRD FICTION

THE THING IN YELLOW, D.T. Neal

REALITY SQUALL, J. Krawczyk

———

SCIENCE FICTION

SINGULARITIES, D.T. Neal

FARTHER, Dean Vale

THE CHARGE OF THE WOLVERHINO, Dean Vale

———

ECO HORROR

SUMMERVILLE, D.T. Neal

RETURN TO SUMMERVILLE, D.T. Neal

RELICT, D.T. Neal

THE DAY OF THE NIGHTFISH, D.T. Neal

———

HORROR

SUCKAGE, D.T. Neal

CHOSEN, D.T. Neal

BLOOD, SWEAT, AND FEARS: HORROR INSPIRED BY THE 1970s
Edited by David T. Neal & Christine M. Scott

SERIES

THE SHUTTERCLIQUE, Dave Neal

BRIGHTEYES
INFERNA
TANTRUM (Forthcoming)
COPYCAT (Forthcoming)
HELLMAIDEN (Forthcoming)
EPHEMERA (Forthcoming)
NEMESISTER (Forthcoming)

THE PLASTIC FANTASTIC, Dean Vale

SIGHTSEER
WHEN IN CHROME (Forthcoming)
THREE-WAY MIRROR (Forthcoming)

THE WOLFSHADOW TRILOGY, D.T. Neal

SAAMAANTHAA • *THE HAPPENING* • *NORM*
LUPINIA (A Wolfshaow Book)

SAGAS OF IRTH, Dane Vale

OF SWORDS & SORROWS • *THE WRATH OF SHADOWS*
THE NIGHT'S VIOLIN • *BEYOND THE IVORY SHORE*
UPON THE SERPENT'S TONGUE • *THE TWILIGHT ISLE*
SONG OF THE SORIANS (Forthcoming)
LADY MIDNIGHT (Forthcoming)
THE IRON KNIGHT (Forthcoming)

GOTHIC & THE SUPERNATURAL

THE UNTIMELY UNDEATH OF IMOGEN MADRIGAL
Grayson Daly

A MOONLIT PATH OF MADNESS
Catherine McCarthy

THE HANGMAN FEEDS THE JACKAL
Coy Hall

CHIMERA
Chinaza Eziaghighala

THE ASTERISK ANTHOLOGY 1 & 2
Edited by David T. Neal & Christine M. Scott

WAX & WANE: A GATHERING OF WITCH TALES
Edited by David T. Neal & Christine M. Scott

Nosetouch Press is an independent book publisher
tandemly based in Chicago and Pittsburgh.
We are dedicated to bringing some of today's most
energizing fiction to readers around the world.

Our commitment to classic book design in a digital
environment brings an innovative and authentic
approach to the traditions of literary excellence.

*We're Out There™

NOSETOUCHPRESS.COM

Horror | Science Fiction | Fantasy | Mystery
Supernatural | Gothic | Weird

www.ingramcontent.com/pod-product-compliance
Lightning Source LLC
Chambersburg PA
CBHW031957180726
48283CB00008B/2467